Hugh Scott has always been fascinated by "spooky things", such as ghosts. "I grew up reading ghost stories, listening to them on the radio and I've had some creepy experiences of my own," he says. It's no wonder that he writes spooky stories himself.

It was in 1984, two years after winning the *Woman's Realm* Children's Story Writing Competition, that he decided to give up his job as an art teacher and become a full-time writer. His first novel, *The Shaman's Stone*, was published in 1988 and several more titles soon followed. These include *Why Weeps the Brogan?* (Winner of the Whitbread Children's Novel Award), *The Haunted Sand*, *A Ghost Waiting*, *Something Watching*, *The Gargoyle*, *A Box of Tricks*, *The Place Between*, *The Camera Obscura* and *The Ghosts of Ravens Crag*.

Hugh Scott is married with two grown-up children and grandchildren and lives in Scotland.

Books by the same author

A Box of Tricks
The Camera Obscura
The Gargoyle
A Ghost Waiting
The Ghosts of Ravens Crag
The Haunted Sand
The Place Between
Something Watching

GIANTS

HUGH SCOTT

For Jessica!
December 2019
Hugh Scott

WALKER BOOKS
AND SUBSIDIARIES
LONDON · BOSTON · SYDNEY

First published 1999 by Walker Books Ltd
87 Vauxhall Walk, London SE11 5HJ

This edition published 2000

2 4 6 8 10 9 7 5 3 1

This book has been typeset in Sabon.

Printed in Great Britain by Cox & Wyman Ltd,
Reading, Berkshire

British Library Cataloguing in Publication Data
A catalogue record for this book is
available from the British Library.

ISBN 0-7445-7292-4

For Jamie,
who is a giant in spirit

CHAPTER ONE

ONE SATURDAY IN OCTOBER

"Stone in my shoe!" warned Harry, and he hopped to a bench and tugged at his shoe. The shoe clung to his heel as if it was happy there, and never wanted to come off!

"Undo the lace!" said Midget and grinned down from his great height. But Harry stuck out his foot and let Midget untie the knot for him.

"Take the shoe off yourself," said Midget. He ruffled Harry's hair as if Harry was his pet dog instead of his little brother.

"Hurry up, you nuisance," said Midget cheerfully. "Don't pretend you can't tie your own lace!"

Harry had been tying his laces for so many years that he couldn't remember not being able to tie them. So he said nothing, except,

"There!" as he finished, and jumped off the bench.

Midget was standing on the grass looking up at the cathedral. He looked like a man rather than a big brother.

"What?" asked Harry.

"Nothing. Let's walk," said Midget.

"People think you're my dad," said Harry.

Midget chuckled. He stopped suddenly, and looked around the grassy square. Harry looked too.

People were walking along the brick paths. A small boy was being lifted by his mum on to the barrel of a cannon which stood as a monument to the town's ancient past.

Harry could see the dark shape of St Margaret's church with trees around it as if to protect it from something.

But Midget was gazing up – not at the church – but at the cathedral, which raised its monstrous tower so high that half the sky was shut out.

"It *is* big," said Midget.

"Bookshop!" urged Harry.

"Yeh, yeh. Bookshop. But take a look, Nuisance. Stop – for goodness' sake – and just *look*!" And he stared again at the cathedral.

Harry stared.

The west tower above him, really was enormous, with gigantic shoulders the size of ordinary churches, supporting it.

When Harry had first been inside one of these shoulders, Dad had said, "You could put *our* church in here with room to spare!"

Dad had meant that the church at home – at Upper Hampton where they used to live – would fit inside one shoulder of the cathedral. And Harry had shivered, because it had seemed to him that mere people – huh! even if they were as strong as Midget! – could never have built so gigantic a place!

And Harry had shivered so much during that first visit to the cathedral, that Midget had carried him (Harry being much younger then) as they followed Mum and Dad among the mighty pillars and stared upwards at the inside of the central tower which seemed as high as the clouds.

Dad had said, "Built by giants," and though he had spoken quietly, his words had bounced like ping-pong balls, whispering into the stone distances, leaving a silence broken only by a faint, tremendous heartbeat which had made Harry bury his face in Midget's shoulder; but Dad had said the heartbeat was the central heating pumping warmth through the cathedral.

"Don't stand there dreaming!" ordered Midget cheerfully. "Off again were you? Always dreaming! Bookshop! Do you want to be carried?"

And Harry frowned at this joke, because he

felt that Midget had got into his thoughts, and had stolen the idea of carrying him.

But Harry knew that Midget couldn't really get into his thoughts. So he ran ahead, dodging round a huddle of corners into Main Street, leaving Midget to follow at his manly pace.

CHAPTER TWO

The bookshop sold second-hand books. The books were on shelves which rose in front of you and behind you and beside you, so confusingly that, once *in* the shop, you wondered if you would ever find your way out!

Harry didn't mind if he never found his way out. He loved the dusty feel of the books. And he breathed the smell that clung to the old cloth covers and to the leather bindings. He enjoyed the light bulbs dangling at odd heights like bright spiders to illumine the titles or scorch your cheek if you were as tall as Midget.

"*Come and see!*" whispered a voice; and Harry looked at a girl whose eyes were suddenly so close to his that if he'd stuck his tongue out, he'd have licked her nose.

Harry had never seen the girl before.

"*Come and see!*" she insisted, and her

brows pulled down so fiercely over the brown circles of her eyes that he nodded obediently.

Instantly she turned and crept among the shelves to where fewer bulbs spread their dangling light, and more shadows dozed.

She stopped and pointed at a gap between the books on a shelf beside Harry, then breathed warmly in his ear, "Don't cry out! Look! Just look!"

Harry looked through the gap into a private part of the bookshop. Books warmed the walls here too, and the same electric bulbs hung high up or low down making bright spots amid shadows; and the brightest spot was over a table where a man (whom Harry had seen often in the shop) sat with a book on his lap.

The man, Harry decided, (wondering what it was the girl wanted him to see), was perfectly ordinary for a bookshop man. Rather dusty, as he always seemed, in his brown suit; and he was eating – though for the moment Harry couldn't see *what* he was eating. A sweet maybe. Certainly not his lunch because there was no plate on the table...

Harry straightened and turned his puzzled face to the girl, but her fingers amazed him by leaping at his ear, grabbing hold and forcing him to peep through the gap again!

Well! Harry was not about to put up with...

But Harry forgot his ear.

The man's hand rested on the page of his

book. His fingers moved as if to gather a corner of the page in order to turn to the next page; but instead of turning the page, the fingers slowly tore the page out crushing it into a ball, then the fingers raised the ball and pushed it into the man's mouth.

Harry gaped.

The man chewed.

Harry glanced at the girl. She nodded grimly. He stared again at the man who chewed as if he had never enjoyed a book so much, then his fingers dragged another page free and stuffed that into his mouth!

"He's a nutter!" whispered Harry with a grin. "A book worm! Ha! Ha! Ha—!"

"Shut up! Come on!" She led him swiftly through the shop.

They passed another man, as dusty as the first, sagging behind a desk, who looked up as if expecting to be given money.

"Sorry," said Harry, as the girl hurried him out into Main Street.

"I wanted to buy a book!" he complained.

He saw Midget chatting to a tall girl. "There's my brother."

"Never mind your brother—" She glanced at Midget. "Your brother? He looks more like your dad!"

"You've never seen my dad."

"He looks as if he *might* be your dad!"

"I *know* what you mean," said Harry.

"What's your name?"

"You tell me yours first!"

"Harry," said Harry in surprise. Why should he have to tell his name first?

"Marty," said the girl. "Now listen…"

"Marty's a boy's name," said Harry.

"Martina! It's short for Martina! Never mind that. Listen will you—"

Harry remembered the man eating the book. "He's a harmless nutter," he said. "He's owned that shop for years. If he was dangerous the police would—"

"Are you new here?"

"What do you mean?"

"Are you new in this town? Have you moved from somewhere else?"

"Keep calm," said Harry. "We came from Upper Hampton. But ages ago. We're not new exactly."

"I don't belong here either." Marty glanced around as if she was the heroine in a spy film. "We can't talk on the road." She grabbed his arm and marched him along busy Main Street.

"Hey, Midget!" yelled Harry.

Midget's head turned, then he spoke to the tall girl as if he was saying cheerio, but Harry shook his head, so that Midget hesitated.

"Through here!" said Marty, and Harry glimpsed Midget still watching, as he let Marty take him through Monks Close – which was an archway of ancient stone, with shops on either side and houses above.

Then, once through Monks Close, they popped into daylight, with the cathedral looming over them, and the grassy cathedral grounds around them and, at the far end of the cathedral, the square where Harry had taken the stone from his shoe.

"We'll sit on that bench!" declared Marty. "Tell me what you saw in the bookshop!"

"*Me* tell *you*? But *you* told *me*!"

"I only got you to look! What did you see? Tell me now!"

Marty's brown eyes stared so hard that Harry felt her gaze was pushing him along the bench.

"I saw a man eating a book!" he said. "What is all this?"

"A man eating a book." Marty's gaze softened.

"Page by page," said Harry. "Isn't that what you saw?"

"Did you see anything else?"

"No. Just books stacked up…"

Marty slumped. She gazed at the cathedral. She said, "Oh, well."

Harry waited. He was puzzled. Marty seemed disappointed that he had seen a man eating a book. What else had she expected?

Marty faced him and grinned suddenly, her smile so plumpfull of such cheerfulness that she seemed like a different girl. "It's better than nothing!" She grabbed his hands.

"Hey."

"I'm glad I talked to you in the bookshop. You're not bad for a boy. Now, listen carefully. You and I must stick together. What school do you go to?"

Harry remembered having to be first to tell his name.

He said, "What school do you go to?"

"Tell me-ee!"

"Martina!" mocked Harry.

"Har-old!" mocked Martina, and she laughed so merrily that her voice returned from the walls of the cathedral in fluffy chuckles so that Harry laughed too, and *his* chuckles came tumbling around both him and his new friend; and together they said, "Partiger's Primary!"

"Partiger's!" repeated Marty. "I haven't seen you there. Mind you, I wasn't in school long enough to see much! Whose class are *you* in?"

"I haven't seen you at all," returned Harry, not answering her question. "Whose class are you in?"

"Aren't kids silly?" laughed Marty, which made Harry raise his eyebrows; he'd never thought of kids as silly – or as anything else. He'd never thought *at all* about kids.

"Miss Jackdaw," said Marty. "Birdie's class."

"Miss Hope," admitted Harry. "She's nice."

"I've only been to Partiger's a couple of times…"

Harry frowned; he didn't really understand that. But Marty went on talking:

"…so I guess that's why we haven't seen each other. Though you're not very noticeable…"

"Hey!"

"I mean, you haven't got red hair."

"I don't want red hair."

"You know what I mean. Will you stop talking rot…"

"I'm not—"

"…and listen? You're the only person I've met who can help. First of all, promise you won't tell, cross your heart and hope to die, spit in the mud, a fly in your eye?"

"I promise. What have I not to tell?"

"About the man in the bookshop, and about…"

Martina gazed at Harry so seriously that he felt cold crinkles walking down his back. Had she something really solemn to tell him or was it just kids' stuff?

Harry was pleased with himself for thinking about kids' stuff; as if he was grown-up.

"What?" he said.

Marty leaned closer.

She drew in a breath to speak.

Harry saw her tongue pop out on to her lip then pop back in; then her eyes jumped away looking at something behind him, and she leapt off the bench and shouted, "Don't you dare call me names! I'll tell my mum!"

And to Harry's amazement, his new mysterious friend turned her back, and ran away sobbing as if her heart was broken.

CHAPTER THREE

Harry knew his mouth had opened in astonishment.

He watched Martina running off around the end of the cathedral. He didn't know what to think.

A footstep crunched beside the bench.

Harry looked up.

A figure towered close to him, so tall that for a moment he thought it was Midget with the sky dazzling down behind him. Then the figure wasn't so tall, which made Harry frown, and a woman's voice said, "You are not displaying bad manners in public, are you Harry? Partiger's has a reputation for well behaved children."

"Miss Hope!" said Harry, and stood up.

"I'll see you on Monday," said Miss Hope, and she sailed past, following the direction Marty had taken round the cathedral.

"See me on Monday?" groaned Harry. "But I didn't *do* anything!"

Then he remembered Marty had been about to speak when...

"...when she saw Miss Hope," Harry explained to himself. "But why did she run away? Why did she not just pretend we were chatting – which we were. Hang on. Maybe she didn't want Hope to know we were friends."

Harry didn't doubt that Marty was his friend even though he had known her for only a few minutes.

"She didn't want Miss Hope to know we were friends."

"Off again?" asked Midget cheerfully, approaching along the brick path which led from Monks Close.

"Just thinking," said Harry.

"That's what I meant."

Harry looked at the girl waiting shyly behind Midget. She was tall, but the shiny top of her black hair only just reached Midget's shoulder.

"This is Jennie," said Midget. "This is the nuisance I told you about. Say hello, Nuisance."

"Hello," said Jennie, and they all laughed at Jennie being the nuisance.

"Hello," said Harry, and he smiled, because he liked Jennie's gentle gaze and her white skin.

"Jennie lives out of town," said Midget. "Had a bit of an upset, didn't you, Jen, and yours truly was the nearest thing to a hero…"

Jennie's face lost its whiteness and turned grey. Harry looked at her in alarm.

"I need to sit down," whispered Jennie. She sat on the bench beside Harry, shivering.

"You need something to warm you," said Midget.

"Put your head between your knees," suggested Harry.

"I think maybe I should," gasped Jennie and she bent forward.

"Bend lower," said Midget. His hand floated as if to push Jennie's head further down, but he hesitated.

"Down more," said Harry, and pressed his hand into her black hair.

Jennie, said, "Oh. Ooh. That's better."

She sat up with her cheeks healthily white, with a dash of pink in them.

"Thanks, Harry. I didn't have breakfast. My mum's always saying—"

"I've enough money for a sandwich," said Midget.

"Oh, I've got money!"

"Can you stand?"

She reached for Midget's arm and stood up.

"You don't mind if I hold on to you?"

Midget shook his head.

Harry sent him a look that said, "I'll bet you

don't mind!" Because she was pretty, was this Jennie!

"It's not far to the coffee shop," said Midget. "You don't know the town, do you?"

"First visit. What a fright. What a terrible thing. Thanks for looking after me."

"You can tell us over a sandwich."

Midget led Jennie towards a gate in the wall which bordered the cathedral grounds.

Harry hesitated, wondering if Marty would come back, and if she had dodged Miss Hope.

He wished Marty's head would peep round a corner of the cathedral; but the cathedral stood like a city, filling the sky, while passers-by followed the brick paths, or walked through the tunnel which was Monks Close.

The gate in the wall, where Midget had taken Jennie, led into a garden.

The garden snuggled around a house almost as old as the cathedral. The house was Harry's favourite place in the whole town, partly because he liked old buildings made of crumbling red brick, but more because he loved coffee with cream doughnuts. He couldn't remember a time when he didn't love coffee with cream doughnuts – which was a bit odd, he knew, because most kids (Harry grinned at thinking of himself – again – as a kid) – because most kids preferred coke to coffee. He went through the gate and into the house, and sat a table with Midget and Jennie.

Midget ordered as if he was grown-up, and Harry waited, watching Jennie's shy face. He was curious about what had frightened her. He had never seen anything in the town to frighten *him* – though he remembered again his first visit to the cathedral, when Midget had carried him to keep him safe from his fears.

"What scared you?" asked Harry; but the waitress delivered cups and plates, so that Jennie said nothing.

"Jennie lives at Lowwater," said Midget.

"Oh," said Harry.

"She's just moved there. I'm at Queen's School," Midget told Jennie. "Behind the cathedral"

"Is Queen's nice? I start there on Monday."

Jennie, Harry knew, wasn't thinking about Queen's School.

"We can take a look if you want," suggested Midget. "It's only five minutes from here, and a bit like this house – this coffee shop—"

"The Almonry," said Harry.

Jennie's eyes touched his, and she said, "What's an Almonry?" But again, Harry was sure she was thinking about something else. Which was just as well, because Harry didn't know what an almonry was.

"A building where the church gave out alms," said Midget, watching Jennie's gentle face. "You know – money for the poor. This house belonged to the cathedral then. Hundreds of years ago. What did you see? What frightened you, Jen?"

CHAPTER FOUR

Coffee arrived, and cakes, with Harry's cream doughnut.

"Are you sure you don't want a sandwich?" asked Midget.

"You know the tunnel we came through?" said Jennie, shaking her head to the offer of a sandwich. "That archway with shops on either side?"

"Monks Close," nodded Midget.

"I peeped through it. From the main road."

"Yes, it's called Main Street."

"I wasn't sure if Monks Close was private…"

"It could seem private if you didn't know it led to the cathedral grounds."

"…so I walked on. Along Main Street. The buildings the shops are in are very old. If you look at the storey above the shops, you can see. Old brick, and stone. Old, old roofs and chimneys."

Midget frowned.

"Old windows," whispered Jennie.

"Did you see something at a window?" asked Midget.

Jennie's fingers prodded her cup. She nodded.

"I saw a face," she said. "You won't believe me. You really won't."

"You were like a ghost," Midget reminded her, "when I found you outside the bookshop."

Jennie whispered, "I saw a huge face! Filling the window! It was turned sideways as if a giant was lying on the floor gazing out at normal people! Oh, I'm freezing!" She grabbed her cup and gulped her hot coffee.

Harry gaped at Midget. Midget puffed out his cheeks silently.

"It must have been something else," said Harry, but he couldn't think what.

Midget asked, "Are you all right, Jennie?"

"The coffee's warming me." She bit her cake. She gobbled it down. "Oh! I feel better. It wasn't anything else. It was a face—"

Harry said, "What about a plastic head that people wear at fairgrounds? You know, the head's as big as the person? And somebody left it at the window for a joke..."

Jennie had shut her eyes.

She opened them. She said, "It was gone when we walked back along Main Street. Me and..."

She stared at Midget. "I can't call you 'Midget'."

"Um, Millingham," admitted Midget. "Millingham Rothwell. Some people at school tried calling me 'Millie' for short, but they changed it to Midget when I advised them it was for their own good."

"Midget," repeated Jennie. "What *was* your mum thinking of? Sorry."

Jennie's white cheeks gathered rose petals as she blushed.

"She called me 'Millingham'," explained Midget, "because it's a family name. I was supposed to have a normal first name as well, like 'John', but she and Dad couldn't agree." He laughed. He shook his head. "Silly story this. They couldn't agree even on the way to the registrar's where babies' names are recorded. So instead of 'John Millingham Rothwell', I ended up just 'Millingham Rothwell'. Story of my life."

Jennie smiled. "The face opened its mouth," she said.

* * * * *

"The face opened its mouth," said Jennie again, "and I thought what you thought, Harry – a dummy head. But it licked the window! It was being deliberately offensive! Then it leered at me!" Jennie stared at the

27

crumbs on her plate, in silence.

Then colour came into her cheeks and she dabbed up the crumbs until they were finished.

Harry said, "*I* saw something weird today." And he told Jennie and Midget about the man eating the book and how Marty had run away when Miss Hope appeared at the bench. "I thought Miss Hope was you at first," Harry told Midget, "because she seemed really tall…" Harry paused, puzzled. "Then she wasn't tall. It was a bit strange. Oh, and another odd thing was Marty asking if I was new to the town. She made it sound really important. She's new to the town. And Jennie's new. I suppose none of us really belong. You saw a giant's face, Jennie. And Marty saw something in the bookshop that she didn't get a chance to tell me about. And I saw the man eating the book. Can being new have something to do with seeing weird things?"

"Hum," said Midget. "You're not new, Harry. You've been here for years. Look, I've got an idea. If everybody's finished guzzling, let's go back to the bookshop and see if anything's happening. And on the way, Jennie can show us the window with the giant's head."

CHAPTER FIVE

Harry, Midget and Jennie emerged from Monks Close on to Main Street.

They walked in the direction of the bookshop, but before they reached it, Jennie whispered, "There!"

Her hands landed on Midget's arm. "The wet streak's still on the glass! Above the toyshop! Look!"

Harry looked. The window was old, made of many little bits of glass which reflected the sky. Yes, he *could* see a clean streak across several of the little panes. But he could see nothing else.

"Walk on," said Midget. "I see it," he assured Jennie. "But there's nothing we can do just now. Head for the bookshop."

Harry wondered if Marty might be around, but the street was busy and he couldn't see her.

They entered the bookshop.

The dusty man behind the desk raised his eyebrows at Harry.

"Thought I'd have another look round," mumbled Harry.

He headed into the depths of the shop, the cliffs of books suddenly on either side of him, Midget and Jennie behind him.

"This way!" he urged.

"Don't rush," said Midget. "If something funny is going on we shouldn't give the game away. Act casual."

"Oh." Harry acted casual. He whistled.

Jennie giggled.

Harry stopped whistling as he wandered around booky corners. He knew that other people were in the shop but in this maze of shelves he might as well be alone. Except for Midget and Jennie.

"Which way?" asked Midget. "Better choose a book."

"I wanted an Arthur Ransome."

"Get it then. We'll head towards the back shop."

Harry found a few Arthur Ransome's that he hadn't read: some paperbacks and old-fashioned hardbacks. He had enough money for three paperbacks or one hardback. Three paperbacks meant more to read, but the hardbacks were thicker and sturdier, and had a dusty, cupboardy smell. The paperbacks were cheap looking.

Harry choose *Winter Holiday* in hardback.

He headed after Midget and Jennie.

He found them chatting comfortably in a corner just large enough for two.

"Cough, cough," said Harry.

"Here it comes," sighed Midget, meaning Harry.

"This way," said Harry.

He sidled around an end of shelves, and found the gap in the books which had let him see into the back shop. The dusty man tearing out pages would have gone by now, Harry guessed. At least – he wouldn't still be eating.

Harry bent and peered through the gap.

Midget and Jennie crowded beside him though there wasn't enough room for them to see.

The dusty man, Harry saw, was standing, reaching up to the top of a pile of books.

The pile of books was stacked high – in fact, they were stacked up to the ceiling where even Midget couldn't reach without using a chair; and the dusty man wasn't specially tall, but...

Harry frowned, so that Midget whispered, "What is it?"

The man's reaching arm extended upwards, and his fingers found a book right on top of the pile and lifted it down.

Harry continued frowning, trying to understand what he was seeing.

The man *wasn't* tall.

31

He wasn't small, either, but no way could he...

"But that's impossible!" yelped Harry, and he found himself pushed aside.

Midget crouched to peer through the gap while Jennie looked at Harry, her face tipped in a question.

Midget glanced up from the gap. "What's impossible, you nuisance? He's reading a book. Is that the same man?"

Harry nodded.

"Let me see," whispered Jennie, and she crouched beside Midget, wobbling, so that he had to steady her with an arm around her shoulders.

"That's all we need," mumbled Harry, thinking of Midget fancying Jennie; but Midget paid no attention, though the tips of his ears turned red.

"What's he doing?" hissed Harry.

"Nothing. Reading."

Nothing. But Midget stayed crouched, Harry noticed, with his arm around Jennie.

Then somewhere in the bookshop, feet pattered, running among the shelves, and a girl's voice said, "Harry! Where are you? Are you here? I've got to tell you!"

It was Marty.

CHAPTER SIX

Harry popped his face around a shelf and beckoned.

"Harry!"

"Ssh!" warned Harry.

Marty stopped when she saw Midget and Jennie crouched at the gap in the books. They stood up.

"This is my brother…"

Marty stared up at Midget's great height.

"…Midget. You saw him in the street. And Jennie. She's new in town—"

"Did you see the bookshop man?" interrupted Marty, nodding towards the gap in the shelves.

"He's reading," shrugged Midget.

"Follow me!" ordered Marty suddenly, and she darted away towards the shop door.

The others found her on the pavement looking around as if spies were on her trail.

"What's up?" asked Harry, sniffing his new book inside its paper bag. "Why did you run away when Miss Hope—?"

"Stay with me!" And off she dashed again, Marty, glancing back fiercely to make sure they were following.

"She's heading towards the square," said Midget cheerfully. "Is she your new friend? When she squeaks – you jump!" He meant that when Marty gave orders, Harry obeyed.

"You're jumping too," said Harry, and he plonked a smile at Jennie, whose quiet face was bewildered.

They followed Marty on to the grassy square with the cathedral tower filling the sky.

Marty ran to the cannon where the mother had put her little boy when Harry and Midget had passed earlier.

"Gather round!" she said. "Hide me!"

"We're hiding you," smiled Midget. "So you're Marty."

"Martina Grenville. I go to Partiger's Primary. At least, I'm supposed to. I only moved to this town a couple of weeks ago and I've been to school just twice! Listen. Things are happening! Miss Hope's one of them…" She hesitated, looking at Midget and Jennie.

Harry opened his mouth to ask who "them" was, but Marty said, "You're really big."

She continued staring at Midget.

Then she said to Harry, "Are you sure he's

34

not your dad? Oh. Sorry. I'm sorry. I'm getting paranoid! Sometimes I think I'm crazy! I guessed I'd find you in the bookshop. Lucky I did. I've given Miss Hope the slip. Tell me what you saw!"

"Books," murmured Midget.

"This is serious!" snarled Marty so fiercely that Midget stepped back. "*You* saw something," she accused Harry. "Tell me!"

"I saw that man. He … reached up." Harry didn't know how to say what he'd seen.

"That's it!" whispered Marty. "He reached up!"

"Up to the top of a great pile of books," said Harry. "Up near the ceiling."

Midget said, "I don't get it? Jen?"

Jennie shook her head.

"The ceiling!" hissed Marty. "The ceiling's way up! Even *you* would need a ladder! Is that right?" she asked Harry. "He reached up further than any ordinary person possibly could reach?"

Harry nodded.

Midget said, "I still don't get it. We only saw a dusty chap examining a book."

Marty said, "I saw him reaching up, too. When I was in the bookshop earlier. I've been hanging around the shops, you know, instead of going to school. Then I saw Harry, and got him to look through the gap. But the man had stopped reaching by then, and was eating the book. I know it sounds mad! But listen! I had to tell somebody what I knew, so I grabbed you, Harry, and ran, but Miss Hope appeared and I didn't want her to know we were friends, and I couldn't let her catch me!"

"Hey," said Midget. "Calm down. We don't know what you're on about. Why have you been hanging around the shops? Why don't you go to school? And why should Miss Hope want to catch you? She's Harry's teacher—"

"Harry's teacher!" snarled Marty fiercely. "Is that what you think she is? And you want to know why I don't go to school? I'll tell you! Miss Hope isn't just a teacher. Miss Jackdaw isn't just a teacher. Maybe none of the teachers are just teachers! I'll tell you what Miss Hope is, shall I?"

Marty glared.

"Miss Hope," she whispered in a terrible voice, "is a *giant*!"

CHAPTER SEVEN

When Marty said: "Miss Hope is a giant!"
Jennie leaned suddenly on the cannon, her face
very pale. Harry knew that Jennie was remem-
bering the giant face at the window above the
toyshop.

But Marty kept talking, until Harry said,
"Miss Hope isn't a giant. Everybody knows
that."

"Oh, listen, listen!" said Marty. "When you
saw the man in the bookshop reaching up, did
he change? Did he turn into a giant?"

"Of course not."

"Yet you couldn't see how he reached so
high?"

"No-o."

"That's what they do. Sometimes they're
ordinary, like Miss Hope. Sometimes..."

Marty sighed.

She gazed around the square.

The cathedral tower loomed hugely, as if, thought Harry, it was listening to their conversation.

"I've a lot to tell you," said Marty. "Can we go somewhere? Miss Hope might come and I want to get out of sight. I want to get warm. I'm really scared." And to Harry's embarrassment Marty took his hand and stood shivering beside him in the cool October sunlight.

They walked away from the cathedral.

They walked towards St Margaret's Church.

St Margaret's Church lay behind trees at the side of the square.

As they strolled along the path to the church door, the trees were between them and the square, which made the cathedral less powerful, but more than ever like a small city rising out of a grassy plain.

Or maybe, thought Harry, like a vast machine that someone had set down on a level bit of ground, and it had lain so long that people had forgotten the time when it wasn't there, and had built houses around it, as they might have built houses in the shelter of a quiet volcano.

"In we go!" said Midget, pushing the church door.

"Is it all right?" said Marty. "Won't the vicar mind?"

"He likes kids," said Midget solemnly, and

Harry smiled.

"It's warm," whispered Jennie. "Is there a heater we can sit beside?"

They found an iron radiator at the foot of a pillar, and Jennie sat next to it in the pew, with Midget close, and Harry and Marty kneeling over the back of the pew in front.

Marty was shivering.

"Did you have any lunch?" demanded Midget.

"He *is* like somebody's dad," said Marty, and Harry grinned.

"*Have* you?"

"No."

"Well, get warm. Don't say anything interesting until I come back."

Midget edged out of the pew and vanished into the depths of the church, and nobody said anything interesting until he came back carrying a plate.

"Couple of buns," he apologized. "I put jam on them." He shuffled into the pew and handed the plate to Marty, who snatched a bun and stuffed it headfirst into her hungry face.

"Where did you get those?" cried Jennie.

"The back shop," grinned Midget. "The vestry kitchen. There's usually more than buns…"

"But you can't just—"

Midget laughed.

"Our dad's the vicar. Didn't you see our haloes?"

He patted Harry on the head.

"The vicar?" smiled Jennie.

"Is that other bun for me as well?" said Marty. "Thanks! Oh. Umph. Gulp. Oh, that's better. I was starving!"

"So," said Midget. "Warmed and fed. Tell us about giants, Marty. How can a bookshop man be a giant, and nobody's ever noticed? And how can Miss Hope be a giant as well as an ordinary school teacher? And just how many giants are there living in our little town?"

CHAPTER EIGHT

Outside the church, not far away, a machine's deep voice growled.

"My dad," said Marty suddenly, "does a conjuring turn for charities."

Harry started to ask what conjuring had to do with giants, but Marty said, "Kids are his worst audience, he says, because they see what he's really doing, while adults see what he wants them to see."

The brown circles of Marty's eyes stared at Harry.

She went on, "I think the ... giants, make us see what *they* want us to see. They make us see what we *expect* to see. The giants are here, but we expect to see ordinary-sized people – so we *do*. But when a new kid arrives in the town..."

"Like you're a new kid," said Midget. "And Jennie's new. And she saw ... wow," said Midget. "No wonder you were going on about who was new to town! Hey, Jen, tell Marty what you saw."

But Jennie shook her head, and let Midget tell Marty about the giant head.

Then Midget said thoughtfully, "But Harry's not new, and he saw the bookshop man..."

"Oh, that's easy," said Marty. "The bookshop man didn't know anyone was watching. So if he thought he was alone he probably wasn't trying very hard to look ordinary. You know – whatever he usually does to look ordinary, he didn't bother doing."

"Gog and Magog," announced Harry, "are alive and living in our town."

"What?" said Marty. "Are you being funny? Do you want to be punched?" She raised a chubby fist.

"You've heard of Gog and Magog?" smiled Harry. "Giants from olden times. Everybody around here has heard of them. They're supposed to walk in and out of the cathedral at night, stretching their arms in the moonlight, terrifying any kids who peep out of their bedroom windows instead of going to sleep. Ooooh!" groaned Harry frighteningly, and Marty's fist landed on his chest.

"Shut it," said Marty, "and listen. This is serious. My mum took me to school the day after we moved to this town. A fortnight ago. You know Partiger's Primary..."

"I don't," said Jennie.

"Well, it's got really high ceilings. My mum noticed that. She said it would be hard to heat. Somebody said the head teacher – Miss Partiger – had insisted that the ceilings should be high when the new school was built, same as the old school – apparently it was ancient – and pals of hers on the local council had agreed.

"High ceilings are convenient if you're as tall as a bus," said Marty. She added quietly, "I saw a giant. Mum had stopped the car at the school gate, and she was fiddling with her seatbelt when I saw it inside the school – coming out of the front door. It had to duck to get out, even though the doorway was really high. Then it came down the steps and was no bigger than anybody else.

"I couldn't believe it, and I didn't have time to say anything before Mum bundled me out of the car, and then I was sitting in a class with other kids and Mum was smiling and waving goodbye.

"Then I had to go to the toilet. Miss Jackdaw said where the toilet was, but I got lost and wandered around until I saw a door with LADIES on it, and used that.

"But I turned a different way when I came out and found I was in the staffroom. It was huge. Far bigger than in my last school, and the walls were nearly hidden by class photos.

Some of them looked really old. But I didn't take a close look, because there was a bar of chocolate on a table. Well, nobody was around and I thought they wouldn't mind sparing a new girl one measly square—"

"You shouldn't steal," said Harry.

"Huh! I didn't. Before I touched the chocolate, I saw that somebody had taken a bite out of it. It was a big bar – you know – *this* long. Somebody had bitten the end off it."

Marty looked at Harry.

"What?" said Harry.

Marty looked at Midget and Jennie. She said to Midget, "That chocolate was thick. Maybe *you* could have bitten through it, but I couldn't. My dad couldn't—"

"Oh," breathed Jennie, "a *giant* bite!"

"The teeth marks," said Marty, "were clear, and they were as big as dominoes!

"Well, I was scared.

"I ran to the staffroom door, but somebody was coming. The only place to hide was under a chair. So I dashed for the row of chairs along the wall, threw myself on the carpet and rolled out of sight.

"And in came Miss Hope's feet.

"Her hand lifted the chocolate bar. She said, 'Mmph', and the wrapper floated on to the table. She must have demolished the rest of the bar in one mouthful. Then she went to the sink, filled the kettle, made herself a cuppa, and picked a book from a bookcase. Her legs wandered closer.

"She sat in the chair I was under, and oh! the seat bulged down so that I thought my head would get squashed! But it didn't quite. Then she leaned back – I heard every move. She leaned back and stretched her legs.

"Her legs grew out across the carpet.

"I'm not kidding you. They grew further out. Remember, this was my first day. I hadn't any idea of giants, really. And I lay still, trying not to shriek, with the seat bulging down over my ear, and the next seat also bulging down as she got wider, I guess, and those legs getting longer and longer – until they stopped! And her ankles relaxed and her feet tipped outwards, as if relieved.

"My poor heart was clattering!

"Then I heard paper.

"I know now, what she was doing. She had scoffed the chocolate, and now she was eating the book that she'd lifted from the bookcase. Goodness knows why they do that, because they eat ordinary food like the rest of us! Chocolate, you know! But all I heard was paper tearing, and an occasional gulp. Then she finished her cup of tea and left the staffroom looking quite ordinary. I got out fast.

"Miss Jackdaw wanted to know where I'd been all this time, so I just clutched my middle, and she nodded, saying I looked pale."

"Why didn't you go home?" frowned Harry. "I'd have gone home. I'm not going to Partiger's on Monday! Midget, you'll tell Dad about this won't you?"

"Calm down," said Midget. "Nobody's been harmed. Kids have been at Partiger's for years without getting hurt. But that was some scare for Marty. Why didn't you go home?"

"Nobody in," said Marty.

"And you went back to school the next day?" asked Jennie.

"Humph!" said Marty. "I did! And it was worse!"

CHAPTER NINE

"I went back to school," said Marty, "because I could hardly believe what had happened. People don't grow legs that cover half the room, and anything might have been used to cut the chocolate bar! I kidded myself I'd been dreaming. Fallen asleep in the loo, maybe. And of course, I didn't tell Mum and Dad! What would they have said?

"So I went to school next morning, ready to run, I can tell you! But no giant appeared out of the front door. I didn't see any grub with huge bites out of it, and I didn't see people reaching up impossible heights, or..."

Marty turned her face away.

She was crying.

"I was thinking," said Midget loudly, "about how huge the cathedral is."

Harry realized that Midget was taking their attention away from Marty's tears.

"Of course," said Midget, "everybody *knows* how big it is! But if you stand and look – just *see* the massiveness of the whole building! I remember our dad saying it was built by giants..." Midget hesitated.

Marty pretended she wasn't crying, and in a moment she really wasn't.

Silence – quite suddenly – filled the church. There was no sound of the machine outside.

Midget murmured, "Somebody's switched off the uprooting gadget. For the trees, you know."

Faintly, Harry heard men's voices.

He recognized his father's voice, suddenly loud, saying: "Oh, what now! Really, I wanted these trees cleared before the frosty weather sets in!"

Then Harry realized that Marty had blown her nose, and was talking about her next day at school, and he listened to her.

"–wandering instead of playing. Not that I knew anybody to play with. I was still puzzled about the day before. I sat under a tree–"

She's in the playground, thought Harry.

"–then the bell rang." Marty frowned with worry. "She must have been thinking about something. Miss Jackdaw, I mean. She must have been thinking really hard about something, because she came out of the side door to call us in – as a giant."

"Birdie's a giant?" said Harry. Then he

remembered that Marty had said that earlier.

"Plain as could be," said Marty. "Tall as a lamp post. But not thin. Big. Big legs with big feet. Big arms and hands–"

"Huge head?" squeaked Jennie.

"Yes. Not *too* big! I don't meant that. She was just big all over. Then she blinked, and I think she realized she had forgotten … forgotten to do whatever it is they do to seem our size. Then she was human. And she looked around quickly, but all the kids were dashing about or shoving each other into line and none of them noticed – or pretended they didn't.

"Then she saw me watching her.

"And her mouth opened. She knew that I had seen her as a giant. She stepped towards me and was half-way across the playground in just two strides – even though she seemed her usual height.

"I scarpered. I ran among the kids. Her arm stretched after me, but I dodged. I knocked some boy down and he wailed. I think she picked him up.

"But by that time, I was off! Out of the playground and along the street. I haven't been back."

"No wonder I didn't see you at school," said Harry, but he was listening again for his dad's voice from behind the church.

"Terrifying," said Jennie to Marty.

"Aren't you listening?" scowled Marty.

49

Midget and Jennie too, had caught Dad's voice carrying irritation into the church.

"Of course we were listening," said Midget. "But something's up. This way, Jen."

He led Jennie from the pew, and Harry – clutching *Winter Holiday* – nodded at Marty to follow him.

They bustled through one or two little stony rooms which normal church-goers never see, then popped out on to grass, gravestones and torn-up earth.

Heaps of sawn trees filled the air with scent.

Two men stood beside a machine which had obviously been tearing a tree stump out of the ground. The men were looking into the hole left by the stump.

"Hi, Dad," said Midget. "What have you found?"

"Hello, Midge," said one of the men.

"Midge?" whispered Jennie. "Your dad looks like a workman. Sorry. Sorry," she giggled, and Midget grinned.

"On Sundays he looks like a vicar. Anything interesting?" asked Midget. "Oh, this is Jennie, Dad–"

"Jennie," said the workman who was the vicar.

"And Marty."

"Hello."

"And this is Nuisance, young Harry–"

Dad hugged Harry.

"We've pulled up a bone by mistake," said Dad. "At least these tree roots did. It's a very old graveyard," he announced to Jennie, "so we got permission to clear the gravestones and trees and let some light in to the church. But we're not supposed to dig anybody up." He frowned and peered into the hole. "I don't understand…"

Harry looked down into the tatters of roots still in the hole. He saw a long bone, as brown as the earth and big enough for the butcher's window.

"What's up?" asked Midget.

"I think we'd better have it out." Dad nodded, and the real workman stepped into the hole and pulled out the bone.

"Careful! Is it a femur?"

"Thigh bone," murmured Midget. "Dad studied medicine before he went into the Church."

"It's rather thick," muttered the vicar, "and no major processes. It's not a femur. More like an ulna in shape, but far too long…"

"Arm bone," said Midget.

"It must be an animal, though the more I look at it…" Harry's dad turned the bone over. He bobbed it about on his palms. "Wuff!" he laughed. "Makes me wonder if the old stories aren't true! Giants…" He shook his head. He said, "If common sense didn't tell me differently, I'd say this was an arm bone from

51

somebody approximately twelve feet in
height."

CHAPTER TEN

STILL SATURDAY – BUT NIGHT

Arthur Ransome slept on the carpet in the darkness beside Harry's bed, tired out after being read for the first time in years.

Harry lay listening to the sounds of the night.

Laughter reached him as people passed from the pub after closing time.

A breeze scraped the fingers of the walnut tree against the house. Harry imagined he could hear the silence which filled the empty space around Dad's church – St Margaret's – which lay beyond the garden hedge; and he imagined he could hear rumblings inside the cathedral – though it was further off across the square – but, still – the rumblings reached Harry's ears from somewhere, as if giants were making deep music in the grey quietness among the cathedral's pillars.

Harry slept.

He woke. Someone had opened the sitting-room door, for he could hear the television. Just the late night news. His thoughts drifted with pictures of things he had seen during the day, and things he had been told. Especially of the giant face leering at Jennie from the window in Main Street. Horrible, that was. And poor chubby cheeks – Marty – squashed under chairs in the staffroom, watching in terror as Miss Hope's legs stretched across the floor. And fancy Miss Jackdaw being a giant too and chasing Marty across the playground!

"...and finally," said the television, "scientists have announced a new principle in space flight through the development of a remarkable new engine. At present, a rocket engine not only has to lift its own weight out of Earth's gravity, but also the weight of the rocket.

"The proposed engine will be shaped like a rocket with crew compartments and everything else required to sustain life, within it. Or, to put it another way, the walls, floors and other solid parts of the spacecraft will *be* the engine.

"Scientists predict that this new type of spacecraft will be virtually unlimited in size, because the bigger the craft, the bigger the engine – and the bigger the engine, the more it can lift.

"The only problem so far is what kind of fuel it will use, because ordinary rocket fuel these days takes up too much room.

"This is Trevor Davenport wishing you a very good night.

"Good night."

"Good night," sighed Harry, and the television was silent. Darkness smothered the land while Harry slept.

Perhaps the people from the pub laughed still, nearer Main Street now, but Harry was safe in his ocean of dreams. Perhaps organ music lingered through the caverns of the cathedral – but Harry's ears heard only the adventures that all kids hear in their deepest sleep. And so what! if scientists have come up with a new idea for spaceships? Harry's travels through dreamland took him into weirder places than astronauts could ever go. And Harry didn't need rocket fuel to follow Dick and Dorothea through their Winter Holiday…

Crash!

Harry sat up, not awake yet.

Had something crashed? He listened to the echo of the crash, wondering if it was an echo of his dream.

He heard Mum's voice. And Dad's: "I'll try not to wake them." No sound from Midget's room.

"Harry?" whispered Dad, as if his head was

round the door.

"What was that noise?"

"Go to sleep."

"Is it a burglar?"

"You know what I think of burglars," said Dad fiercely.

"Mum says you'd give a burglar a cup of tea."

"Is that so? Sleep."

Dad's presence withdrew. Harry lay down, listening.

He heard his father's footsteps returning. Harry asked, "Is it a burglar?"

"No. A cup fell off the fridge. Shouldn't have been there. You know how the fridge vibrates. Good night, Harry."

Harry closed his eyes.

He was startled as Dad's bristly kiss landed on his brow.

"Hmph," smiled Dad in the darkness.

"Mmm," replied Harry cheerfully.

*　　*　　*　　*　　*

THE NEXT DAY, WHICH WAS SUNDAY

The local radio station was broadcasting as Harry bounced into the kitchen for breakfast.

He accepted a passing kiss from his mum whose hands carried scrambled egg on plates, and a friendly kick from Midget even though he was sitting miles away at the far side of the table – he really did have long legs!

Harry leaned on Dad at the top of the table for his hug.

"Listen!" said Dad, and raised his eyebrows at the radio.

"…as they sang their way home through the cathedral grounds…"

"Somebody killed?" asked Mum.

"Nearly. Last night…" Dad's fingers spread, asking for hush.

"…missed the four revellers by a hair's breadth. Mr John Jacob said he felt the draught. And the thud – as it hit the grass – sobered him up. On examining the object they discovered it was the top of one of those pretty, fancily carved pinnacles which decorate the highest points of the cathedral, and from the ground look as if they weigh no more than paper.

"A spokesperson for the cathedral said this particular bit of stone weighed, in fact, nearly two hundred kilos – that's over four hundred pounds to those of us who didn't leave school yesterday…"

"Could have killed the four of them!" frowned Dad.

"It wasn't even windy last night," said Mum. "Eat your eggs while they're hot."

"The tree was scratching my wall," said Harry.

"Coming to get you!" boomed Midget quietly.

Harry smiled. "It was just a breeze," he said.

"They do keep the cathedral in good repair—" began Dad.

"Listen, Dad!" Midget bent towards the radio.

"This report from Gary Jones, our science correspondent. Gary, what's all this about an earthquake?"

"Not an earthquake, exactly, Tim, but an earth tremor. It wasn't serious, and did no more than shake a few plates out of cupboards..."

"Our cup!" said Harry.

"...and it could explain your fallen pinnacle, Tim. But this tremor was felt up to fifty miles away, which is most unusual, and definitely not expected by our scientists, though it appears that several minor tremors have occurred over the last week or two, but they were so slight that only the sensitive instruments at the Royal Observatory could pick them up. Even someone at the epicentre – which was just about on your doorstep, Tim – would only have thought that a heavy lorry was passing. That shows how little we have to be worried about. Scientists say they are expecting no more tremors for at least five hundred years. So you have plenty of time, Tim, to finish this morning's breakfast show."

"An earthquake!" said Mum.

"What's an epicentre?" asked Harry.

"The middle of the tremor," said Midget. "At least, the surface of the earth above where the tremor starts inside the ground. The further you get from the epicentre, the less power there is."

"Well, the radio station is just off Main Street," said Dad, "and the report said the epicentre was close by, so it couldn't have been far from here."

"Midge," said Mum suddenly, "be a dear, and see that we haven't lost any chimneys. In a house this age…"

"And cracks in the wall," sighed Midget. "Back in a minute. Though I think we'd have heard a chimney falling. I could eat another egg," he said, as he left the kitchen; which was his way of getting paid for looking at the chimneys.

"I'd better move," said Dad. "Are you coming to the morning service, Harry?"

"I thought I'd go and see Marty," said Harry. "If that's all right."

"How far away does she live?"

"Nightingale Road."

"Oh, I know it. What? Ten minutes to get there?"

Harry nodded.

"OK. But either phone your mother from Marty's, or report back here. Marty could stay to lunch?" he asked Mum.

"Of course," smiled Mum.

"Thanks, Dad," said Harry, and he rushed
to his room to pull on outdoor clothes.

CHAPTER ELEVEN

Marty answered the door of her house in Nightingale Road.

"You've been crying," said Harry.

"I know. I saw you coming." She nodded upstairs. "I'm not allowed out."

Harry opened his mouth to ask why not, but Marty said, "I told my mum that I hadn't been to school. She walloped me. She says she'll take me right into the classroom on Monday. Tomorrow."

Marty sat on the doorstep. Harry sat beside her. "What did she say when you told her about the giants?"

"Nothing much. Did you tell your mum and dad?"

"Midget said we shouldn't worry them," said Harry.

"Because they wouldn't believe you," sighed Marty. "I don't blame them."

"What does your dad say?"

"Oh, he says it's mum's job to sort me out. I don't need sorting out! I need help!"

To Harry's surprise, Marty wept suddenly.

He patted her shoulder.

He couldn't think of anything to say.

At last, Marty stopped crying. "I'm scared."

"Uh," said Harry. Then he said, "My mum says you can come for lunch."

"I'm not allowed!"

"Ask. Tell your mum who my dad is."

"Oh, the vicar!"

"Of St Margaret's."

Marty smiled from her damp face. "Might as well have a go." She ran into the house.

"And tell her," called Harry, "that I'll keep an eye on you at school!"

"OK!"

Marty returned smiling. "I've to wear something decent and have a shower first, but I can come!"

Harry grinned. "Go on then."

"You've to meet Mum."

Harry went in.

Marty had vanished upstairs. Harry went in alone to a sitting-room.

Marty's dad lowered the *Sunday Times*, managed a smile and glanced at Marty's mum, who took over.

"Hello, Harry."

"Hello."

"Sit down."

Harry sat.

Marty's mum smiled. She was tall and pretty. She said, "Did you hear about the earthquake?"

"We lost a cup," said Harry.

"We didn't notice," smiled Marty's mum. Mrs Grenville. That was her name.

"A bit of stone fell off the cathedral," said Harry.

"Yes. Nearly killed some people! Do you live near the cathedral?

"Not far. Across the square. My dad's vicar of St Margaret's. Our house is over the hedge from St Margaret's."

"Oh, that lovely old brick house! I know it. We would have bought your house if it had been for sale. We only moved here a couple of weeks ago. Marty was so naughty not going to school. I don't understand—"

"She was scared," explained Harry. Surely Mrs Grenville could understand that.

"Giants," said Mrs Grenville.

"That's right," said Harry. He saw Mrs Grenville smiling as if he had told her a fairy story, then she met his gaze and her smile changed to a solemn look.

"Don't tell me," she said, "that you believe it? I mean, Marty doesn't tell lies as a rule, but to expect—"

"It's true," said Harry. "Jennie saw one in a

house in Main Street. Jennie's my brother's friend. And my dad dug one up."

Marty's mum stared at Harry, then nudged her husband.

"Mm?" said Mr Grenville to his *Sunday Times*.

"Dug one up?" repeated Mrs Grenville.

"Yesterday. Behind the church. Behind St Margaret's. The graveyard hasn't been used for over a hundred years, and everybody said it was untidy, though I liked it because the gravestones were all tumble-down with trees everywhere and bushes to hide in."

"What do you mean, your father dug one up? A giant?"

"He didn't mean to. The machine pulled a tree stump out, and we found a huge bone…"

"Oh." Mrs Grenville sounded relieved. She smiled.

"My dad used to study medicine."

Mrs Grenville looked interested.

"He said the bone was an arm bone–"

"Then I expect it was–"

"–but whoever owned it must've been twelve feet tall. What's that in metres? Here comes Marty!"

Marty thundered into the sitting-room, beaming, and wearing a skirt.

"We're off, Mum! Dad! See you later!"

"Phone me from the vicarage."

Marty's mum waved from the front door,

her face puzzled. But Harry smiled as he waved back. She would understand once the idea of giants sank in. Grown-ups always were a bit slow with new ideas.

CHAPTER TWELVE

Harry pushed open the back door of the vicarage and went inside. "Mind those baskets of vegetables," he warned Marty. "Kitchen's full of them."

"What are they all for?" asked Marty.

"Harvest Festival."

Harry heard his mum's telephone voice piercing the house.

"I think that's them now, Mrs Grenville. Harry? Is that you? Is Marty with you? Yes, Mrs Grenville, they're both here, though I expect they'll disappear until lunch time... Harry's very sensible for his age... Midge may go with... Oh, yes, most odd. It must have sounded strange coming from a little boy, but my husband's quite perplexed by it...

"He kept saying last night that it must be an animal bone, but it sounded to me as if he was trying to persuade himself... I'm sure that in his heart he is *certain* it's human...

"Gog and Magog. One can't ignore the possibility. A real Gog *or* Magog. God certainly springs surprises on us..."

"Let's go," said Harry. "She'll be ages on the phone. WE'RE OFF MUM!"

"...Excuse me. One o'clock for lunch!"

"Right!"

Harry and Marty scampered out of the back door.

Something soft landed on Harry's hair. He shook the something on to the path.

"Moss," said Marty and they looked up on to the roof.

"What-ho, Nuisance," grinned Midget. He was astride the roof, balancing a bucket and wielding a trowel. His heels rubbed more moss from the red tiles. "Found a crack round the base of this chimney pot. I don't think the earthquake caused it. Too old." He sighed cheerfully. "Somebody's got to glue the family home together. Hi, Marty. Saw you arriving, but I was kind of busy hanging on up here. Where are you off to?"

"Around."

"Know it well," said Midget, aiming a trowel-load of cement at the base of the chimney pot. "Lot of hoogle-bumps there. Watch out for them. See you later."

Harry and Marty ran.

Marty shoved Harry.

Harry shoved Marty so that she yelped.

Marty grabbed Harry in the middle of running, so that he had to run in a circle until he bumped against her, and they fell. Fortunately they were in the square by then, and the grass was friendly to falling kids.

Marty dashed towards the cannon and clambered up its wheel, then sat on the barrel. She jumped down. "It's freezing, that metal, when you're wearing a skirt."

"I'm not wearing a skirt," said Harry and ran (it seemed to Marty) up the wheel and along the barrel. He sat on the barrel. "It *is* cold," he admitted.

"You went up there like a monkey!" cried Marty. "You ran up the cannon!"

"Oink, oink!" grinned Harry.

"That's not a monkey!" scolded Marty.

"Eek!" said Harry, and stepped off the barrel – which was higher than Marty's head, and she gasped, but Harry landed and dashed away as fast as a bouncing ball.

"You're like a bouncing ball!" shouted Marty, and Harry stopped running. A bouncing ball. That reminded him again of his dad saying the cathedral had been built by giants; when his voice had bounced like a ping-pong ball among the pillars.

He said, "Let's go into the cathedral."

"OK," said Marty. Then: "Let's find that stone. The one that nearly killed the drunks!"

"Yeah!" cried Harry, so they ran across the square and on to the flat grass around the cathedral, and there was the stone.

No one was looking after it.

From a little distance away, it seemed as if it was made of curls of grey paper.

When Harry and Marty got close, they could see that the papery curls were, of course, curls of stone, one lapping behind the other, like fancy waves on a frozen ocean.

"It's as big as me," said Marty. "See how deep it is in the grass. Wham!" She leaned back and gazed up.

Harry gazed up.

"Some drop," said Marty. "Can you see where it came off?"

Pinnacles of curly stone stuck up everywhere on the cathedral tower.

"Not really," said Harry. He blinked into the autumn sunlight.

Then he sat on the stone.

Marty leant on a ledge which ran along the monstrous wall of the cathedral. She frowned.

Harry asked, "Are you worried about going back to school tomorrow?"

She nodded.

"I was thinking about that," said Harry on his stony perch. He noticed a beer can at Marty's feet – dropped by those people last night, he thought, when the stone fell.

But he said, "I don't think there's anything,

really, to worry about. Midget said the giants have never hurt anybody."

"You haven't seen them," mumbled Marty. "*Giants!*" she whispered.

"But I've seen Miss Jackdaw and Miss Hope and the head teacher!" cried Harry. "I was in Miss Jackdaw's class when she taught younger kids. Miss Hope's my teacher now. They're nice."

"They're *giants*!"

"Even if they are…"

"Well?"

"They're nice."

"Huh!"

"But just think. They've never harmed anybody. Miss Hope never shouts. And you said yourself that Miss Jackdaw picked up the boy you knocked down in the playground – when you were running away from her."

"That doesn't mean—"

"It *does*! Don't you see? *You* didn't pick him up—"

"She was after me!"

"–but *she* did. She was after you, but she let you go so's to pick him up. She wasn't *desperate* to catch you…"

"She knows where I live," mumbled Marty.

"But she didn't go to your house. A whole two weeks, and she didn't report you or go to your house. And when Miss Hope followed you round the cathedral—"

"I was scared."

"But *she* wasn't desperate to catch you either, was she?"

Marty thought. "Well…"

"Listen, if they *were* desperate, why didn't they lie in wait at your house? They could have got you any time. Why didn't they phone your mum and kick up a fuss and get you back to school?"

Marty scowled.

Harry said, "Because they really weren't worried about what you knew. That's what I think, anyway. I think they understood you were scared, and they were giving you time to get over it."

"No. They—"

"It must have happened before. People seeing them, I mean. They know how to handle it. I expect grown-ups who see them by mistake – if nobody does anything – just persuade themselves that they imagined they saw giants."

Harry watched Marty.

Her mouth screwed itself around uncertainly.

"Maybe," she admitted at last.

Her foot found the beer can.

"Huh," she said, "it's full." She picked it up. "You want to taste it?"

"No way!"

Marty held out the can, and fizzed open the

ring-pull. She put the can to her mouth.

"Yug!" she cried. "Lager! It smells awful!" And she dropped the can, and the two of them, Marty and Harry, gazed idly at the lager pumping from the can on to the grass close to the wall of the cathedral.

Marty was talking.

"...I said, let's go into the cathedral. Harry!"

But Harry was seeing something curious. He was seeing something very curious indeed.

CHAPTER THIRTEEN

"What are you looking at?" demanded Marty.

Harry eased himself off the stone pinnacle and crouched at Marty's feet.

The lager had spread through the grass, leaving bubbles on the stems.

Harry pointed at some stems of grass beside the cathedral wall. The stems were curved over – a whole bunch of them – making a little grassy tunnel that a mouse, perhaps, could hide in.

"Is it a nest?" asked Marty, crouching at Harry's knee.

"They're all bent over."

Marty stood up. "Let's go into the cathedral. I've never seen inside. Here's somebody coming to look at the pinnacle."

A woman approached, carrying a cardboard box overflowing with fruit and canned food. She looked at the pinnacle. She gazed up at the tower. She looked at Harry and Marty.

She saw the beer can.

She said, "Humph!" and marched away.

"She thinks we were drinking it!" protested Marty.

Harry didn't care what the woman thought, and used a gentle finger to try to pull the grass straight. It was odd...

The grass refused to straighten; so he pressed it flat, half expecting a mouse to run out. But nothing ran out, and Harry peered.

He frowned.

He said – with a bit of a shiver, because really, this was more curious than he'd first thought.

He said, "The heads of the stems are under the stone. The heads of the stems," he said slowly to make it clear to himself, "are under the cathedral wall."

"It's the Harvest Festival," said Marty. She was on the pinnacle, balancing. She nodded towards the brick paths that led to the cathedral door. People were carrying boxes and baskets and flowers. Cars had stopped where they shouldn't, and families were lifting pumpkins and armfuls of carrots, and more boxes, and heading towards the cathedral door – which was out of Harry's sight, round the corner.

"I hope we do as well," he said, thinking of St Margaret's which he could see through the trees beyond the square. "Let's go in, then!" And he and Marty headed round the corner of the tower and joined the people entering the cathedral.

They had no money to put in the glass case that waited for donations; but nobody said anything. Everybody was too busy sightseeing, with brochures to read, or asking where they should put their boxes of harvest festival gifts.

The gifts were displayed between the pillars, making colourful splashes amid the greyness of the vast building.

"Smell the fruit," said Marty.

"I smell dust," said Harry. "I can smell the fruit, too. Look." He nodded upwards.

Autumn sunlight spread in through windows very high up, like spotlights across a gloomy stage. The beams of light seemed filled with fog. "You're right," said Marty. "The air's full of dust. I wonder where that came from. Maybe it's always dusty."

"Maybe," said Harry. He hadn't been in the cathedral since his first visit, so he didn't know about dust. It seemed odd.

Like those curved-over grass stems.

Harry shook his head. *That* really *was* odd.

But Marty was pointing out a gigantic peach-coloured pumpkin, saying, "...paint a face on that and you've got Miss Jackdaw! Right size, anyway!"

Harry smiled. Miss Jackdaw did have a

roundish face, but it was nothing like a pumpkin. He'd always liked Miss Jackdaw's face. He always thought that she seemed ... wise. Yes. Miss Jackdaw looked at you *wisely*.

Harry shook his head again. Surely Miss Jackdaw couldn't really be a giant...?

TA-RA-LEE! shrieked the enormous voice of the cathedral organ.

"Oh!" yelped Marty.

"It's loud!" complained Harry. "Let's see where it is!"

They walked until they left the harvest behind, and stood under the central tower which soared as high as the clouds. Harry remembered that, just here, was where Dad had first mentioned giants.

"There's the organ," said Marty, and advanced towards the organ pipes, which were like a bundle of telegraph poles with their mouths open, and painted gold; but too high up and too half-hidden among stone archways for Harry and Marty to get close.

"Try this way," said Harry, and they walked until they found themselves behind the archways which hid the organ. And immediately, they found a little stone staircase spiralling up ("Narrow for a giant!" grinned Harry) and, at the top of the staircase, someone's head swaying to the throb of the music.

Marty held her ears, laughing at the noise thundering and trembling around them.

Harry touched the staircase, and he nodded eagerly at Marty to touch it too, for though the staircase was built of stone, it vibrated with the blast of the organ.

Then Marty made a face at Harry, her glance pointing him towards a space under the staircase; and Harry stepped closer, and found an open doorway packed tight with darkness.

He thought: This would take us under the organ. Under that huge wall of archways that the organ is built into. Does it go down? he wondered, under the ground? And he stepped in without thinking, and discovered another curious thing.

CHAPTER FOURTEEN

The entrance did not take Harry under the ground. His feet stepped on flagstones which led him straight inside the huge wall. It seemed to Harry that the wall was hollow, though he could see nothing in the darkness.

He reached out on either side, so that one hand dug into the darkness to touch emptiness, and his other hand touched...

"What's this?" said Harry.

"Where are you?" whispered Marty, her voice was right at Harry's shoulder, or he wouldn't have heard her for the shouting of the organ.

"Feels like cardboard boxes," said Harry. "Some of the shopkeepers give us whole boxes of tinned peas maybe, for the Harvest Festival. This feels like tinned peas."

"So it does. Stacked up. This feels like tinned spaghetti," chuckled Marty.

Harry smiled. He looked towards the entrance. The gloomy daylight inside the cathedral peeped in after him. Marty was a black shape between him and the light. And the light shone dimly on the cardboard boxes nearest the door. Stacked up, right enough. Stacked higher than Harry could see.

"Can you read what it says?" he asked Marty, because she was nearer the light, and she peered at the boxes. "Beans," she read. "Peas, right enough. Steak and kidney pud. Tinned carrots. Sausage. Boiled potatoes…"

"Boxes of tinned food," said Harry, feeling further into this dark place within the wall. "It's all boxes as high as I can reach." He stepped away from the boxes in the direction where his hand had touched emptiness, but one step took his palm on to stone.

"A stone wall at that side," he said.

"Which side? Oh, I feel it!"

"And boxes at this side. Is it all food? It can't *all* be for the Harvest Festival." He was walking forward as he spoke. He looked back at the entrance which now seemed half its original size. And the organ boomed only faintly, protected as they now were inside the wall – though when Harry touched the stones he felt them tremble. He wondered at the amount of energy in the noise of the organ – so much energy to make these gigantic walls shake in their shoes!

And on he walked, with Marty's little fingers on his back, and the cardboard under his hands, and now the smell of cardboard in every breath, and the cathedral trembling around him.

* * * * *

Harry stopped walking. Before him, the darkness in this strange corridor danced with green lights, but Harry knew these were the lights which everybody sees when no real light is around.

"We've come far enough," said Marty, as if agreeing with Harry having stopped.

"We're at the end of the boxes."

Together they felt the cardboard wall beside them. They felt round the end of the wall of boxes. For a moment Harry thought the wall turned a corner because his fingers found more boxes, but he realized that it was simply another layer of boxes behind the ones he had felt his way along – in other words, the wall was two boxes deep.

"Hundreds of them," said Harry.

"Thousands!" whispered Marty.

"Yes. Thousands of boxes of food."

"Let's go back."

The entrance was now a slot of pale light floating in the blackness.

"I can't hear the organ at all," said Marty.

Harry touched the stonework. "You can still feel it." As he spoke the trembling in the stone stopped, and the silence was suddenly more silent, and Harry knew that the noise of the organ had been going on around him, but so low and mysterious was its sound that his ears had scarcely heard. Only because it had ceased did he recognize the real silence that now filled this dark place deep inside the cathedral.

Suddenly, he too wanted to get out. He did not like this silence! And finding one more curious thing – a store of food too enormous to be Harvest Festival food – also disturbed him. He remembered that you *display* Harvest Festival food! You don't hide it away in a secret place!

"Let's go!" Marty's breath landed on his face.

"We can't go, Marty," said Harry gently. "Somebody's shut the door."

CHAPTER FIFTEEN

Marty's feet pattered on the flagstones. She was running back towards the door.

Harry could see nothing but darkness, but he ran after Marty, his fingers touching the boxes so that he would run in a straight line.

Ahead, he heard a bang like a fist on a wooden door and Marty yelled, "You've shut us in!"

Harry slowed to a walk until his hand found Marty's shoulder.

"I thought I could catch whoever shut the door," she gasped. "But they didn't hear me. The door's solid. It's like hitting a tree."

Harry felt past her. The door was cool and made of wood with iron bands holding it together. St Margaret's had doors like this.

He said, "At least we won't starve." He was talking about the boxes of food – though really he was thinking about the door. Some of the ancient doors in St Margaret's had no lock. He found a coiled ring of metal which was the door handle.

He said, "I'll bet you a pound we get out." And before Marty could reply, he turned the handle and pulled.

Light leaned in.

"Oh!" gasped Marty. "I thought…"

Harry opened the door further and they went out under the spiral staircase.

He turned and shut the door. He knew what Marty had been going to say; he didn't like the idea, either, of being locked in that dark place inside the cathedral wall.

He led Marty swiftly among the smells and colours of fruit, and through the taste of dust.

Into the sunshine they went, where people were still delivering Harvest Festival gifts.

A van was parked on the path, with Miss Hope unloading boxes from its rear, on to the grass.

Harry grabbed Marty's arm. He said, "She hasn't seen us! This way! While she's leaning into the van!" He led Marty to the front of the van.

The van driver was at the back, helping Miss Hope to unload.

"…wasn't expecting any more," Miss Hope was saying. "I've just this minute shut the door. It's a long journey… Three years, even at our speed…"

Harry pushed his eyebrows up. Three years? No journey takes three years! Why, you can fly round the world in a day or two...

"...and who knows what we'll find when we get there after all this time... I'll be sad to leave, won't you? But we knew it would happen one day, when too many people found out about us. No, I'm not crying, thank you. We really should get these boxes under cover before anybody wonders..."

"What does she mean?" whispered Marty. "Even at their speed? And if she's going somewhere, why pack provisions into the cathedral? All this van-load can't be for the Harvest Festival! They must be putting it beside the food we found! Isn't that Jennie coming?"

Jennie was strolling from the direction of Main Street. She waved, and Marty waved at her to hurry.

Jennie walked faster until she stopped beside them at the van.

She said, "Are you hiding? Is it a game? Hello, Harry."

"Hello—"

"It's not a game! It's Miss Hope taking boxes from this van!"

"It's the toyshop van," said Jennie uneasily. "Same writing on the side as above the toyshop in Main Street. I passed it again just now, coming from the bus station. Midge asked me to meet him at the cannon."

"She's storing great stacks of food in the cathedral!" said Marty.

"Miss Hope?" asked Jennie, her white, gentle face puzzled. "It's the Harvest Festival—"

"No! It's all hidden away."

Jennie was gazing across the square towards the cannon. Harry knew she was only half-listening to Marty.

Harry said, "Here's Midget. Midge," he grinned. He waved, and Midget ran easily across the grass and stopped, smiling down on everybody – Jennie's black hair above her happy glance, as high as Midget's shoulder.

"Hello, criminals," said Midget. "Thinking of hijacking the toyshop van? If you wait till Christmas I expect Santa—"

"Mi-idge," ogled Harry, shutting him up.

Midget grinned, and explained to Jennie: "Up until now, only Dad called me Midge."

"Will you shut up about your name!" exploded Marty. "And keep your voices down! The cathedral's stacked with food – don't say it's for the Harvest Festival! Something's going on. Miss Hope's at the back of this van with the driver…"

"No she's not," said Midge, smiling at Jennie. "I could see as I crossed the square – just you three looking suspicious."

"Then she must have gone inside. Come on. Don't ask *her*!" cried Marty, as Midge opened his mouth towards Jennie. He gazed at Marty in surprise.

"This is serious!" declared Marty. "Come on! Into the cathedral!"

"The small ones are always the loudest," said Midge, as he followed Marty towards the cathedral door.

"I'd love to see inside," said Jennie.

"Hold on," said Midge.

"What?" demanded Marty.

He nodded back at the van. "D'you think they want any more boxes taken in? We could carry some. You could manage one box, Harry?"

"Yes," said Harry. "But—"

"It won't hurt to do a good turn. Come on. Back to the van. The rear doors are shut. Not locked, though." He swung the doors open. "Help yourselves. Stewed beef. Can you lift that, Jen? You nuisances take these…"

"I can't meet Miss Hope!" howled Marty. "She tried to get me yesterday!"

"She didn't try very hard," said Midge. "Grab these string beans and stop behaving like a child. Oh."

"What?" grumbled Marty.

"Speak of the devil," said Midge.

Walking towards them from the cathedral, was the driver of the van – and with him was Miss Hope.

CHAPTER SIXTEEN

Miss Hope stepped among them, the van driver looking over her shoulder.

Miss Hope, Harry thought, was the most ordinary person he had ever seen. Her face was ordinary. Her hair was ordinary. She was no taller than his mum. How could she possibly be a giant?

Then he noticed Marty edging away, as if she was going to run, but Miss Hope didn't threaten. She didn't seem upset. She simply raised her eyebrows, looked at the open doors of the van and at the boxes about to be carried off.

"We thought we'd bring these inside," said Midget. "Give you a hand. I'm Midget – Midge – Harry's brother. I think you know Marty…"

"Slightly," said Miss Hope.

"Jennie's from out of town."

"I see," said Miss Hope. And Harry thought she sounded sad at hearing this. She said, "A lot of people have come from out of town recently. Not that I mind, of course, but it can get rather ... overwhelming." She blinked, as if she realized that probably no one knew what she meant. "I just mean…"

She turned to the van driver, but he shook his head.

"I just mean, that too much change in one's life." She laughed as sadly as she had spoken. "Thank you for helping. Please bring the boxes this way."

They brought the boxes, Miss Hope and the driver carrying one each, everybody going ahead of Harry, as he gripped *his* box tightly to keep it from slipping.

Jennie glanced back at him as they approached the cathedral door. She let Harry catch up. She let him go into the cathedral first.

She didn't follow, so he said, "I thought you wanted to see inside?"

She nodded, her mouth looking as if she was about to taste her least favourite medicine. She hefted her box of stewed beef. Her face was paler than usual.

"It's that driver," whispered Jennie as she stepped into the cathedral.

"What about the driver?" asked Harry.

"I've seen him somewhere before! I don't like him! But I only came to town for the first time yesterday, so where *could* I have seen him? We'd better keep up."

Midge and Marty were striding far down the aisle after Miss Hope and the driver.

"Why can't we pile the boxes here?" panted Jennie. "I didn't know that stewed beef was so heavy! How can I have seen him before?"

They followed the others into the centre of the cathedral.

Harry saw the bundle of telegraph poles which was the organ. He had guessed where the boxes were going. They weren't part of the Harvest Festival. They would be stored inside the wall beneath the organ.

Harry and Jennie found Midge and Marty dumping their boxes beside the spiral staircase.

Jennie lowered her box to the floor, and said, "I'm glad that's over!"

Midge took Harry's box, and Harry stood panting. What a long walk from the van to this quiet spot beside the staircase! Miss Hope, Harry noticed, and the driver, weren't panting at all, and neither, of course was Midge. Midge, Harry reckoned, could have carried *four* boxes without panting!

"Thank you all very much," Miss Hope was saying. "I won't ask you to bring any more…"

"Good!" breathed Jennie in Harry's ear.

"Why not?" asked Marty, and she flung a glance at Harry. "We could help you display them. Cut the tops off the boxes and stack the cans—"

Miss Hope was shaking her head. "The morning service will be starting soon. Thank you, anyway, Marty. We'll see you at school tomorrow?" Miss Hope smiled.

Marty didn't. "Oh," she said. "Tomorrow." And she grabbed Harry and led the others through the cathedral until they stood outside on the path. "She didn't want us to see all the food stacked up inside the wall!" she growled.

Jennie said, "I know I've seen that van driver before!"

"Here he comes," said Midge.

The driver passed them with a smirk.

"He's locking up the van," said Marty. "Why is he smirking?"

"They'll take the other boxes in later," said Harry. "For their three-year journey."

They watched the driver returning, smirking still and going into the cathedral. Harry noticed that the bells of St Margaret's were calling people to church. His dad would be gulping a cup of coffee before starting the service.

Midget ran, suddenly, into the cathedral.

"Hey!" said Harry.

"What's he up to?" frowned Marty.

"He looked annoyed," said Jennie.

"Do you mean about that man smirking?"

demanded Marty. "That driver? I'll bet Midget's gone to give him a talking to. Who does he think he is? He's just a beastly toyshop owner. Jennie, what's the matter? She's going to faint! Help her Harry! Stay on your feet, Jen!" ordered Marty. "Come and sit on the grass. You're whiter than a spook. Sit here. She's forever falling over!" exclaimed Marty unreasonably. "Are you ill?"

"No," panted Jennie. "I got a fright. I recognized the van driver. It was *his* face I saw. You mentioned the toyshop, Marty. It was his face I saw leering down at me. But it wasn't a human face. It was the face of a *giant*!"

CHAPTER SEVENTEEN

"Here's Midge," whispered Jennie.

"She fainted," announced Marty.

Jennie leaned on Harry and he helped her to stand.

"Nearly," admitted Jennie to Midge. "That driver's one of them. He's the giant I saw above the toyshop!"

"Calm down," said Midge. "I think it's coffee time. Let's go home. Dad'll be in the church, and Mum will be getting ready to join him, so we'll have the place to ourselves."

"All right," agreed Jennie. She clutched Midge's arm, and they headed across the square. Marty took Harry's arm, but he shrugged her off, horribly embarrassed.

Then he saw she was laughing at him.

She was laughing (Harry guessed) because she was relieved to have got away from Miss Hope; and Harry was relieved that Marty wasn't serious about taking his arm, and that felt so good that he shoved her, but the next thing he knew was Marty pushing him down on to the grass, with her chubby laughter dropping about his ears!

"Come on, you two!" called Midge.

So Harry got up, and they ran, shoving and nudging until they reached the vicarage – that ancient brick house over the hedge from St Margaret's church, with new cement around the base of one chimney – and a woman on the front step, talking to Harry's mum.

* * * * *

Harry's mum's Harvest Festival hat, was set over one ear, artificial fruit bouncing loosely as she shook her head at the woman.

"I really am in a hurry!" Mum was explaining over the clang of the church bells. She saw Midge. "Oh, here are the children! This my son, Midge…"

The woman turned and gazed up at Midge. Then she smiled, as if pleased that Midge was so tall.

"…and Harry. And…"

Midge said, "Jennie. And Marty. Newcomers," he told the woman, and her smile died. She looked familiar to Harry.

"Miss Beagle," said Mum, nodding at the woman. "She's interested in the bone your father found. You know. In the graveyard…"

"We know the bone, Mum," said Midget, staring down at Miss Beagle. "I've seen you around, Miss Beagle," said Midge.

"Miss Beagle owns the toyshop…" Mum moved aside, and Harry saw a box of toys on the doorstep, and he knew why Miss Beagle seemed familiar – he had seen her often behind the toyshop counter, and also – she looked like the driver of the van who had smirked at them only a few minutes before! "She brought these for the Harvest Festival."

"My brother and I," said Miss Beagle, "thought we should contribute to your Harvest Festival."

Harry said, "But you go to the cathedral. Why should you bring toys to St Margaret's?"

"Harry!" said Mum. "Please excuse—"

"But Harry's quite right," said Miss Beagle, her smile trying to warm itself on Harry – but Harry just waited, not smiling.

"It's, um, our duty to share…" She turned to Mum, suddenly, and said, "Perhaps I could just take a peek at the bone, Mrs Rothwell. I've always been *so-o* keen on fossils…"

"You go on, Mum," said Midget, stepping around Miss Beagle. He lifted the box of toys and pushed it into the woman's arms. "Follow my mother. She'll show you where these go," he beamed. "Into the house, you three. That's it…"

"The bone—"

"It's a bone, right enough," agreed Midge. "Straighten your hat, Mum–"

"Oh."

"–but it's not a fossil, so it won't really interest you. Thank you for the toys."

"But when I said, 'fossil' I meant—"

"Better hurry," cried Midge, and he stepped back on to Harry's toes in the hall, and shut the door. The voice of the bells was softened by being shut outside, along with Miss Beagle.

"Wow!" sighed Midget. "Through you go. Kitchen! Lead the way, Harry, you miniature nuisance. What a cheek! I recognized her straight off. Remember the Scrabble that Santa brought down your bedroom chimney last Christmas?"

Harry growled at his big brother.

"She sold it to me. Sit around the table. Mind your head on the beams, Jennie. Some are a bit low just where you are. You're tall for a girl." Midge gathered cups.

"Our family comes from around here," said Jennie, as if that explained why she was tall.

"Ri-ight." Midget blasted water into the kettle.

"My dad says that this area is famous for tall families," continued Jennie. "My dad's nearly as big as you. He's one point eight-nine metres, which is about six-foot three…"

"Our dad's from around here too," said

Midge, "though he's not quite my height. Mum isn't. She's just normal. Except for her hat."

Jennie smiled.

"Now!" cried Midge, sitting on a chair so suddenly that everyone jumped. "What was I doing in the cathedral?"

"In the dust," murmured Harry.

"In the dust," agreed Midget.

"What *were* you doing?" demanded Marty. "Jen was jolly frightened…"

"Having a word with the driver."

"Smirky Face!" scowled Marty.

"Exactly. Smirk, smirk. I didn't like that. I couldn't think why he was smirking. And all this business about giants was annoying me. I haven't seen a giant. I have to rely on you kids – I don't mean you, Jen – and, well, it's hard to swallow…"

"Didn't you believe *me*?" asked Jennie, her face as white as her cup.

"Well, um-tum tiddle-um," said Midget, and he grinned, and Harry watched him as he teased Jennie. "Difficult, you know, just what a handsome chap like myself should think of a girl he's never seen before, collapsing into his arms in a busy street…"

"I didn't collapse! I felt… Oh. You're teasing," she smiled.

"I'm teasing. But I really wasn't sure about your story. Keep calm, Jen. Be reasonable. I'd

96

never seen you before."

"All right." Jennie nudged her cup. "I haven't had any coffee yet."

She met Midge's glance, until a slow grin arose between them.

"OK!" Midge leapt up and attacked the coffee jar with a spoon. "I'm trying to tell you what happened in the cathedral. I slipped in after Smirky Face, and it took me a minute, don't y'know, to catch him because he shot up the aisle as if he was on roller blades, though he didn't *seem* to be walking fast..."

"That's what they do!" whispered Marty. "Because they only *look* as if they're our size. They're giants with giant legs."

"Anyway." Midge served coffee. "Drink up. Biscuits, biscuits, biscuits!"

"I'll get them!" groaned Harry, and got them, and everyone grabbed a biscuit.

"I did catch up with him," said Midge, "and he stopped and stared for a second, then smirked again. You know – as if he knew something that nobody else knew. And I said, 'I've got a giant's bone.' I don't know what made me say it. It just seemed the right thing. And it *was* the right thing. His smirk fell off on to the floor–"

Marty giggled, and Jennie smiled.

Harry waited.

"So I said, 'An arm bone.' I showed him the length of it–" Midge measured the air with his

97

palms. "'As long as my thigh,' I said. Well, didn't he gape!"

"Tiddle-um," murmured Jennie.

"Exactly! Tiddle-um! He could hardly speak. 'Where?' he says. 'Where what?' I says. 'Where's the bone?' he says. 'In my dad's study,' I says. 'Where did you find it?' he says, and I says, 'You can't find things that ain't lost!'

"Then I scarpered, because he was wavering – one second he was smaller than me – next, he was head-high among the stone archways – though only for a second. I didn't wait to tell him that a bone isn't *lost* – in my opinion – if it's buried in a proper grave. I mean, the bone didn't fall out of somebody's arm and get *lost*, the way you'd lose a pen…"

"We understand!" cried Marty. "Doesn't he go on?"

"Don't you get it?" said Midge.

"Get what?" Marty pulled her face into a chubby stare. "Thick, I am."

"The van driver is Mr Beagle–"

"Miss Beagle's brother," said Jennie. "The woman who brought the toys."

"That's right," nodded Midge. "And wasn't she interested in that bone?"

"She was!" agreed Marty.

"And how did she know about it?" asked Midge.

Eyebrows went up, including Harry's. What

was Midge getting at?

"Her brother," said Midge, "the van driver, must have told her – after I told him."

"OK," said Marty.

"But – you dim, lowly nuisances – I had only *just* told him! Then I came out of the cathedral, and we all crossed the square."

Harry knew, suddenly, what his big brother meant.

Harry said, "You had just told him about the bone, but Miss Beagle got here before we did!"

* * * * *

"So Mr Beagle phoned her from the cathedral," said Marty, "because he knew she was interested in old bones."

"Giants' bones," agreed Midge. "But how did she get here so fast?"

"Seven-league boots!" chuckled Marty, "She shot over here while we were fooling about in the square. I *told* you they move at a terrific speed! So what did she really want? Just to see the bone?"

"No idea," grinned Midge. "But it's interesting that they're interested. Isn't it? Pretty anxious she was, to clap eyes on it."

Harry said, "She only brought the box of toys as an excuse. It was really the bone she wanted to see. But even if it is a giant's bone, what difference does that make?"

"Might be proof," guessed Midge.

"Yes, but we've *seen*—" said Harry.

"That's just kids' stories. Sorry, Jen. But we're all just kids as far as grown-ups are concerned. Can you see the police, for example, or the government, doing something because *we* said we'd seen giants? Ho, blooming ho!

"The giants aren't *that* worried about *us* seeing them, but if our dad, Vicar of St Margaret's, presents a bone that the Science Museum can measure and fiddle about with – well! Next thing you know, men in white coats would be digging up the cemetery and listening to local folk-lore. *Then* somebody might believe that we've seen giants, *then* think of the fuss! GIANTS IN OUR MIDST! GIANTS ALIVE IN ENGLAND! GIANTS GET OUT!"

"EQUAL RIGHTS FOR GIANTS," suggested Jennie.

"Huh," said Midge.

"They've never done us any harm," said Harry, thinking of Miss Hope who always spoke quietly in class.

"You haven't had one chasing you through the town!" humphed Marty, and Harry said, "Aow," as her toe kicked his leg under the table.

"What was that for?"

"You. It was for you!"

"Was it!" cried Harry, and scuttled round

the table, but Marty's little palms pushed his face, his arms, his hands, so that he couldn't grab her. And because he didn't want to be pushed over *again*, he retreated to his chair and ate more biscuits "to keep them from going mouldy".

The talk, then, (of course!) was about giants and school, and digging up graves and space-ships with new engines and earthquakes that shouldn't happen but did, and fancy eating books!

The day faded away pleasantly, divided by lunch cooked by Harry's mum.

St Margaret's chimed every half-hour, until Jennie said she should catch her bus home as she was starting at her new school tomorrow. So Mum drove them all to the bus station. Then she drove Marty home to Nightingale Road.

Then back to the vicarage, and the day closed its eyes, lowering darkness over the town, turning the cathedral into a silent city which dissolved into the nothingness of night; Sunday night.

And the darkness lay in the square, moving occasionally as if a breeze blew part of it across the grass; but no one saw the darkness move, for everyone slept.

St Margaret's chimed three o'clock in the morning.

The darkness moved out of the square and

stood among the trees which surrounded St Margaret's church.

Then the darkness put its feet close to the hedge which kept the old graveyard out of the vicarage garden; then over the hedge the darkness stepped, and it stood whispering, its voices level with the mossy vicarage roof.

CHAPTER EIGHTEEN

Harry opened his eyes and stared at his bedroom ceiling. Even on the blackest night, a glow came from the sky to build a faint cage of light around his bed.

Harry breathed contentedly. That cage of light was comforting when he woke to the loneliness of a sleeping house. He touched the pages of Arthur Ransome. He had read another happy chapter before putting his light out.

He closed his eyes.

But as he closed them, the light changed, and he opened them again, quickly, and frowned.

His cage of light had darkened as a shadow bent over him. Then something large, outside, darted away; but so swiftly, that Harry wasn't sure if he had really seen it – and, after all, as he looked around his room, the cage of light was as friendly as ever.

Harry relaxed.

His eyes closed.

Something bumped on the roof and rolled down the tiles. Harry stretched his eyes wide, and pushed back his bed covers.

He shivered. The night was chilly.

He tiptoed to the window, and went on shivering as he looked into the garden. But he might as well have kept his eyes shut for all he could see down there!

"It's just black," Harry told himself.

He looked at the hedge and it too was black; and beyond the hedge, the hunched shape of his dad's church slept silently.

It was funny, thought Harry, how the sky was always paler than things on the ground.

Then the shivers which were walking over his skin shook his muscles, for – quite clearly – between Harry's window and the hedge, a gigantic shape rose out of the garden and moved as if it was walking stealthily round the house.

Before Harry could shout for Midge or press his astonished nose to the glass, a second shape reared up and followed the first, and Harry knew why his friendly cage of light had changed – he knew that a giant had looked in at his bedroom window!

"Two giants!" gasped Harry, and he gripped his pyjama jacket tightly around his chest and shivered, unable to think what he should do.

Then he realized he was scared.

How often had Marty said that she was scared? and Harry, really, hadn't bothered. The giants, he had told her, never hurt anybody. Miss Hope never shouted. Eating books isn't dangerous to others.

But Harry still shivered with cold and fear, because giants who appeared to be normal size, and spoke in friendly voices during the day when lots of people were about, were not the same as tall black shapes with arms long enough to bump carelessly on the house roof and let moss run down the tiles.

No. That was not the same at all.

Harry dashed to his bedroom door. He opened the door with as little creaking of its old hinges as he could manage. He ran to Midge's room. Midge's door lay open. Midge's window faced another side of the house. For a second, a shadow passed across the glass. Then it was gone.

"Midget! Midget!" whispered Harry. "Midge!" He shook his big brother.

"What?"

"Giants! Wake up! Outside!"

"You're dreaming."

"No –"

"Then I'm dreaming."

"Oh! Wake up! I think they're after Dad's bone!"

"Eh?" Midge rolled onto his side. "Eh? Dad's bone?" He swung out of bed. He lifted his dressing-gown from a chair and put it on.

"Where's your dressing-gown?"

"I forgot."

"You're a pale shuddering blob in this darkness. I don't know why it has to be dark every night!"

"Mi-dget!" Fancy joking at a time like this!

"Fumble around for my jumper."

"But the giants—"

"Here it is. Put it on."

"But the giants! I saw them! Umph!" said Harry, as the jumper muffled his head. He pulled the jumper down. "Do something!"

"I'm looking out of the window. I don't see anything. You stay here. I'll take a wander round."

"I'm not staying!"

"Stay here!" Midge's warmth brushed past Harry in the dark. Harry followed. "Aren't you going to waken Dad?"

"Stay!" ordered Midge, and his voice was lower-off-the-ground than usual, because he was half-way down the stairs. "Oh, woof!" muttered Harry. He felt for the top step and descended after Midge. He followed him to the front door.

"You're not going out?" he demanded.

"Are you still upstairs?"

"Yes," lied Harry.

"I'm going round the house. It may not be giants…"

"I saw them!"

"Not in the dark, you didn't."

"I saw them against the sky!"

"It might," said Midge, "be ordinary burglars. Did you think of that?"

"Ordinary burglars can't look in my bedroom window upstairs!"

"Stay!" ordered Midge again, and this time Harry stayed.

Midge's jumper was a comfort, but Harry was still shivering, and his feet were freezing. He put one icy foot on top of the other.

He blinked out into the darkness. Street lights spread a glow which showed Harry the outline of trees in the garden and the hairy shapes of shrubs. But how dark it was! and colder than ever on the doorstep, and hardly a star in the sky, and Midge prowling in this blackness looking for giants.

"Midge!" whispered Harry.

Harry stood still, preventing himself from shivering while he listened.

But he heard nothing, so he shivered again.

"Boo!" whispered Midge.

"Oh! Beast! Did you see anything!"

"Great dollops of nothing. Not a sausage. My feet are icicled!"

"Mine too."

"Let me shut the door. Don't wake Mum

and Dad."

"What are you going to do?"

"Sleep," said Midge, and this time his voice was as high up as a giant's because he had reached the top of the stairs.

"But the giants?" said Harry. He ran up the stairs. "I saw them."

"Maybe. There's nothing out there now. Maybe you dreamt them."

"Oh," said Harry.

"Good night."

"'Night, Midget," said Harry, and he trailed to bed and lay shivering, holding his frozen feet in his hands until Old Man Sleep should carry him to the land of dreams.

But Harry didn't reach the land of dreams.

CHAPTER NINETEEN

Harry suddenly thought of the giants being able to deceive his eyes.

If they can appear small like us, he thought, maybe they can appear to be shadows or bushes. Why, Midge could have pushed past them in the dark! That means the giants are probably still in the garden! because they had come, Harry was sure, for the bone; and since they hadn't got the bone...

"They might be trying the back door at this minute!"

Harry shot out of bed. He was still wearing Midge's jumper. This time, he juggled his feet into his slippers and rescued his dressing-gown from the carpet. That was warmer.

He would go himself, he thought fiercely, and sort out those giants!

He ran to his bedroom window. The garden frowned at the weight of darkness which filled it, but nothing rose up against the night sky.

Harry rushed silently downstairs and looked out of the dining-room window, then he looked out of the lounge window – in fact he looked out of every window except one – and that was the study window. Dad's study.

Where the bone was.

And because the bone was there, the giants would eventually be there too, peering in at the bone on the desk, wondering how to get at it.

Harry stood outside the study and breathed deeply because his heart was dancing rather too cheerfully.

He listened at the door.

He heard only silence.

He opened the door and eased himself in.

He frowned towards the window, prepared not to yell if he saw two giants' heads filling the glass.

But only darkness filled the glass.

Harry walked nearer to the window. His foot bumped a pile of books which had climbed off an armchair to make themselves comfy on the carpet.

"Silly things," whispered Harry.

He stood hiding inside the curtain, peering outside. Now he could see the church resting its head in the clouds.

He jumped as the church clock clanged half-past three, and his heart leapt into a jig. Surely the noise of the bell would waken Mum and

Dad and Midget!

But nothing stirred in the house.

The clang faded, and Harry's heart took a rest. He listened to the trees whispering.

Harry knew that trees whispered when a breeze blew.

He found with his eye, a leafy twig sticking out against the sky. Harry waited to see the twig moving in the breeze. But the twig stuck out perfectly still.

"But the trees are whispering," breathed Harry.

Then he realized that the whispering was louder, and closer. It wasn't the trees which were whispering.

A shadow slid across the window.

Harry opened his mouth to cry out, but he didn't cry out.

"*I see it!*" said the whisper.

Another shadow filled the window, and Harry stood inside Dad's curtain, his heart knocking, wanting to know why he had stopped breathing.

"*Where?*" asked a second whisper.

"*On the desk. Among these books and papers.*"

"*Is the window locked?*"

Something fumbled at the glass. Harry risked letting his eyes move.

A gigantic hand was trying to push the window open.

"*Locked.*"

"*We must get it!*"

"*Must we?*" Harry decided this was a woman's whisper. She said, "*I still say that we should leave as soon as possible! Waiting another week for the earth to reach her precise orbital point is not necessary.*

"*By that time the Reverend Rothwell might establish that the bone is a giant's bone, and people will begin to investigate! Though,*" she added, "*they'll never know it was poor Magog's.*"

"*Miss Hope,*" said the second whisper, "*told us to get the bone.*" A man's voice.

Harry thought that maybe it was a smirky voice, like the toyshop man's. And the woman's voice was anxious like the toyshop lady's – Miss Beagle.

Miss Beagle was speaking.

"*…how we ever managed to forget where he was buried! I know it's a thousand years and more since he died, but… Oh, we should have buried him deeper! I told Miss Hope at the time that we should bury him deeper so that no one could ever dig him up!*"

"*Now, now,*" said Mr Beagle. "*People were watching, remember. We dared not do anything extraordinary or they'd have guessed we were different. We weren't so good then,*" sighed Mr Beagle, "*at holding our shape.*"

"*We're not so good now! People have seen*

us! And you deliberately let that girl see you from the upstairs window in the toyshop! Just for the fun of giving her a fright!"

"All right, all right," grumbled the man. "At least I've kept the engines in order for you. Haven't I?"

"I suppose so."

"Suppose nothing! That latest test last night was perfect! We rose fully eighteen centimetres off the ground, which is two centimetres more clearance than we need for full thrust!"

"Oh yes, yes! So you've worked a miracle with the engines. But we wouldn't be leaving if you hadn't let that girl see you!"

"That's not fair," whispered Mr Beagle.

"No. I'm sorry. So many newcomers now, for us to influence. It was bound to happen. A thousand years. I feel as if this is home."

"Our real home is waiting for us."

"And our children?" said Miss Beagle.

"They must stay here. You know that. They couldn't survive the journey. And with their short life-span..."

"Oh yes. I don't suppose many of them would want to come. You know what Miss Hope said," sighed the woman. "'When they are afraid, they destroy. And they are always afraid of what they don't understand.' She is so right. Our children will destroy us if we don't leave. One day, perhaps, we will come back..."

"*If we don't get that bone,*" said Mr Beagle, "*we might never leave! Let me try the window!*"

Harry had listened so hard, that again, he'd forgotten to breathe.

As the window shook, he breathed.

He gasped.

What should he do?

Yell for Midge? But even Midge was no match for two giants.

Get into bed beside Mum and Dad, and cuddle under their blankets?

Fight the giants himself, letting courage and daring win over size and strength?

Harry still hadn't decided what to do, when the window groaned, and flew open, hitting Harry as it swung back like a door.

Then through the window reached a hand. Even in the darkness he could make out its gigantic size.

"*Ssh!*" whispered Miss Beagle.

"*I'm not making a noise!*" whispered Mr Beagle; and the hand hesitated as he spoke. Then he reached in further towards the bone on the desk.

Dad's desk.

Dad's bone.

Nobody had the right to take Dad's bone. And while Harry Rothwell was around, nobody was going to be *allowed* to take it!

Not even a giant!

Suddenly, Harry knew what to do. The giants didn't know he was there. They knew, he guessed, that Midge had walked around the house earlier, and they now thought, Harry decided, that everyone was asleep.

They certainly were *not* expecting to be disturbed! *They* didn't want to be discovered!

Therefore…!

Harry stepped away from the curtain. He trod silently towards the study door.

If he could reach the door before that hand got to the desk with the bone on it…

He stopped. His slippered toe had bumped against the pile of books. The books grumbled, and Harry crouched and grabbed them.

He looked at the window. It was blacked-out by the giant head of Mr Beagle. Mr Beagle's hand had stopped reaching. Had he heard the books?

Harry balanced the books silently and in three steps he was at the door.

He had left the door open when he came in, so he stepped round it, took a deep breath, and *switched on the study light*!

*   *   *   *   *

Harry pushed the door wider as he switched on the light. He made a pretend yawn as he wandered into the room, blinking as if he was blind with sleep. But he wasn't at all blind with

115

sleep. He saw the giant hand slide swiftly away – without the bone.

Harry tried not to smile.

He peered along dad's bookshelves as if he was choosing a book. He put on a shiver as if a draught was making him cold – which it was – and turned towards the window. He raised his eyebrows on finding the window was open. He could see only blackness outside in the garden, and he tried not to see anything else. He kept his eyebrows showing his surprise while he walked towards the window.

He leaned out.

He looked left and right into the blackness. He saw two tall columns of darkness but pretended that he hadn't noticed. Then he shivered theatrically, and closed the window and fastened it.

As he turned his back on the glass, he felt that two giant faces were looking in at him. He simply knew it. He knew it, as surely as he knew … that he was getting scared again.

More scared.

Yes, more scared, for though Miss Beagle didn't sound fierce, Mr Beagle wasn't so pleasant. Mr Beagle might get violent!

But Harry forced himself to walk to dad's desk, rather than obeying his legs which wanted him to run away. Then, smiling to himself (though still scared!) at the expression he would see on Mr Beagle's face if he dared look round, he lifted the bone, switched off the study light, and fled upstairs!

Harry lay on his bed panting. The bone lay beside him. He kept his arm on it. He smiled as he panted. He chuckled, and his chuckle reminded him of Marty because she chuckled. What a laugh they'd have tomorrow at school when he told her about *this* adventure!

Then the bone vanished. Harry's chuckles vanished, and Harry vanished.

He was asleep.

CHAPTER TWENTY

Harry woke to the bustle of the house on a Monday morning.

"Where did I leave that bone?" Dad's voice floated up the stairs. "Midge, did you move the…?"

The bone was still under Harry's arm. He was still on top of his covers wearing his dressing-gown with Midge's jumper under it. When he landed out of bed on to the carpet he discovered that his feet were still in his slippers.

"Did you dust the bone, dear?" Dad was calling to Mum.

Harry bumped down the stairs. He plonked the bone on to the kitchen table among the morning dishes.

"Oh, there it is," Dad said, as he wandered in. "I was sure I'd left it on my desk."

"You did, Dad," said Harry, and got his hug. He suffered a kiss on his cheek from his mum as she passed.

Midge was watching him from across the table.

"I rescued it from the giants," said Harry.

"Did you?" said Dad.

"Everything ready for school?" asked Mum.

"Yes, Mum. They came last night to get it. That woman who held you up on the doorstep, Mum–"

"I didn't get time to put my hat on straight!" laughed Mum, pouring milk over Harry's sugar puffs. "She was very persistent–"

"She's a giant."

"Persistent about what?" asked Dad.

"Why, about the bone! She seemed quite desperate to see it."

"They came last night!" repeated Harry. "Miss Beagle and Mr Beagle." He nodded at Midge. "You told him we had the bone."

"You told someone – ?" began Dad.

"Sorry, Dad. I told him, because... Well, I wasn't sure why at the time. Yesterday, it was. I wanted to take the smirk off his face, I suppose. But there was another reason."

"What could that have been, dear?" said Mum, sitting down at last.

"I think I wanted to see what he'd do."

"He sent his sister here to get the bone," said Harry.

"Really," said Dad. He frowned. "Well..."

He laughed across the table at Mum. "Giants."

"*You* said it was a giant's ulna, Dad," Midge reminded him.

Dad stared at the bone on the table.

"Yes…"

Mum lifted the bone and took it out of sight.

"Miss Beagle said they should leave," said Harry, "even though the earth wasn't at its…" Harry tried to recall the exact words, " …precise orbital point. But Mr Beagle really wanted the bone—"

"Precise orbital point?" said Dad.

"The earth's orbit?" said Midge through his cornflakes. "You heard her say that? They're leaving the earth? But that means they come from…" He glanced at the ceiling.

He murmured, "The earth must have to reach a particular point in space before they can take off. They really come from *out there?*" His spoon splashed down on his plate. "Of course they do! It's the only thing that makes sense! Well done, Harry! What else did they say? Are you sure you weren't dreaming, you nuisance? I went all round the house, remember."

"They pushed the study window in," said Harry.

He ate his sugar puffs, waiting.

Midge got up and left the kitchen.

He came back, and sat down.

"Well?" asked Dad.

Mum looked at Midge.

"The window's bent," admitted Midge. "Pushed in from outside. What else did they say?"

"The bone belongs to Magog."

"Magog!" whispered Dad.

"They buried him ages ago. Miss Beagle said more than a thousand years, but they forgot where. She said she remembered telling Miss Hope at the time–"

Dad stared at Harry.

"That's what she said," insisted Harry. "She told Miss Hope at the time that they should have buried him deeper, but people were watching and they didn't want to do anything out of the ordinary. Or Mr Beagle said it. He said they weren't very good at holding their shape then."

"And the bone? Why did they want it?"

"They were frightened of what would happen if people found out." Harry scowled, trying to remember. "Something about people attacking what they didn't understand."

"That's true," said Midge.

"Um," agreed Dad.

"And something about leaving their children behind because they wouldn't survive the journey."

"Children!" gasped Mum. She grabbed the teapot and poured Dad's tea. She poured her own, splashing it into her saucer. "Oh dear! Really? Children? Giant children? I've never seen any giant children."

"She sounded quite sad about leaving them." Harry looked at the kitchen clock. "I'd better go!"

"Yes," said Mum.

"Do your teeth," said Midge vaguely to Harry.

Harry dashed off to dress. He did his teeth. He grabbed his schoolbag and popped into the kitchen.

"I've just remembered. Mr Beagle said he'd tested the engines. See you later!" And he rushed through the garden, and ran across the square.

He kept running all along Main Street, but he didn't see anyone in the bookshop which was still shut this early in the morning, and he didn't see anyone in the toyshop which was also shut.

He wondered if Marty would be at school.

Partiger's Primary lay beyond the other end of Main Street, not far from the Almonry coffee shop.

As usual, kids were arriving – mainly out of cars. Harry saw Marty closing a car door. He recognized Mrs Grenville in the driver's seat, and he waved. Mrs Grenville waved back. She opened the car window. "Make sure she behaves!" she called.

Harry nodded, and grinned because Marty was blushing.

The school bell rang and they lined up, Marty in Miss Jackdaw's class line, and Harry in Miss Hope's.

Teachers who taught the younger kids appeared, and ordered their classes into the school.

Harry's line waited.

Marty's line waited.

All the others had gone in, and Harry felt that the teachers had forgotten his class and Marty's.

Shoving started.

Chatter shrilled among the girls.

Harry raised his eyebrows at Marty. Where was Miss Hope?

And where's Miss Jackdaw? shrugged Marty.

Harry thumbed towards the school door, and Marty cried, "Go on in!" to her line – which was pretty cheeky for a new girl.

"Let's go in!" shouted Harry, and braver souls in his line went in, and the less brave followed, dumped their outdoor clothes on pegs, and wandered into the classroom area noisily.

Harry said, "Quiet! Quieten down!"

The class quietened. Harry said, "Something's up."

"How do you know?" challenged a fat boy.

"Because I've got more brains than you. I'm

going to find out!"

"I'm coming!"

"So am I!"

"Me too!"

Harry said, "No," and they stopped. "You'll just get a telling-off, milling about. Wait here and keep the noise down. If a teacher hears you she'll give you work."

He left, glad that his class were hidden by shelves and walls from the rest of the school.

He wanted Marty.

He walked through the school as if a teacher had sent him on an errand. He headed for Marty's class. The noise from there could have been worse, but it quietened when he went in.

"Where's Miss Jackdaw?" asked a girl.

"Um… You've to stay here and keep quiet." Harry used the same trick that had worked on his own class. "If you don't keep dead quiet you'll be given a big pile of writing to do. Marty Grenville's wanted."

"Who wants her?" demanded the girl.

Marty hurried out after Harry.

Harry said, "*I* want you. Watch it. There's Miss Stone. She's going in to your lot."

They heard Miss Stone giving the class work to do.

Harry and Marty busied themselves lifting paints and brushes from a shelf as Miss Stone passed.

"She looks upset," whispered Marty.

"There's Mrs Allington. And Mr Jacks. Where are they all going? Keep behind the shelves."

Miss Stone said, "Have you given the children plenty of work?"

The other teachers nodded.

"It's time to go," said Miss Stone.

"She's crying!" whispered Marty.

So were the other teachers. They all looked around as if they would never see the school again. They walked slowly towards the exit.

"Is Miss Hope there already?" came Mrs Allington's voice. "And Miss Jackdaw? And the head teacher?"

"Warming the engines," said Miss Stone faintly.

Then they were gone.

Only children's voices gave life to the school.

"Where are they off to?" said Marty, getting up from behind the shelf.

"I don't know," said Harry so solemnly that he found Marty staring at him.

She said, "Do you know something? Do you know where they're going? Tell me!"

"I don't know where they're going. But I think they're leaving for good. They're leaving the earth."

Harry's stomach suddenly felt bad. He was hurt that his teachers were leaving.

"Leaving the earth?" whispered Marty. "Are you crying too?"

"They're not coming back," gulped Harry. "Last night … Miss Beagle and her brother tried to steal the bone. But they didn't get it. Now they're leaving because we've found out about them and they're scared of what we'll do."

"Scared of what *we'll* do?" cried Marty. "We wouldn't do anything! I don't know them, but they seem all right for giants! Who would do things—?"

"They're scared of what people will do," said Harry. He didn't try to explain. His eyes kept pushing tears on to his cheeks. He really liked Miss Hope – and to think she was never coming back!

"Let's have a look in the staffroom," said Marty.

"What?"

"We might find out something. Oh, come on!"

Harry followed Marty to the staffroom.

They knocked.

But no one said, "Come in."

Harry gulped. His stomach felt less churny. He followed Marty into the staffroom.

"It's a bit of a mess," commented Marty.

"They've taken stuff with them," said Harry. "Books. Photographs. I'm sure there were photographs on these shelves."

"There were lots of class photos on the walls," said Marty. "I remember thinking how many there were when I hid in here. Really old, some of them."

"See this," said Harry. He had lifted a book. Only the cover remained – an old-fashioned cover, too tough for chewing comfortably. "All the pages have been torn out."

"I can hardly believe that they eat books."

"Paper," said Harry, as if it didn't matter. He nodded towards a newspaper on a chair.

They stared at it without touching it. It wasn't a whole newspaper. It was the remains of a newspaper which someone had bitten.

Then Marty said, "Look at that painting." They gazed at a painting which hung on the wall.

"Miss Jackdaw paints like that," said Harry.

"I've never seen a tree with those sort of leaves."

The tree was certainly peculiar.

The person standing beside the tree was a slightly comical version of Miss Partiger, the head teacher. She was smiling, and pulling bark off the tree with one hand, and pushing it into her smile with the other.

"Something's written underneath," said Marty.

"'Our dear leader'," read Harry, "'enjoying a snack at home. One day we will return, then no more pages from books!' What does that mean?"

They stared at the odd tree, and read the words again.

"I get it," said Harry at last.

"What?"

"Paper's made from trees. That tree must be something they like to eat – like we like Mars Bars. Only these trees don't grow here, so they eat paper instead." Harry sighed.

He felt like crying again.

CHAPTER
TWENTY-ONE

Harry and Marty left the staffroom, and found the school jingling with voices, and kids bustling about.

"What do they think they're doing!" shouted Marty. "Go back to your classes!" But her cry was lost in the din.

"Yes, go back!" yelled Harry. "You can't run around all over the place!"

No one heard Harry either, but suddenly, the voices stopped.

Faces looked at each other, startled. Tears appeared.

"The floor's trembling!" whispered Marty.

"Another earthquake?" said Harry. He shouted. "Get outside!" And kids ran, shrieking and pushing towards the doors. "Take your time!" bellowed Harry, thinking how like a grown-up he sounded; but in a minute, the school was empty.

Pencils rolled off tables.

A globe of the world shook itself to the edge of a shelf and smashed on the floor.

A window splintered suddenly, and stayed quivering in its frame.

"We should get out too!" said Marty, so they ran out into the playground. Some children were standing together, whitefaced, or crying.

"You'd best go home," Marty told them.

"The ground's shaking!" wept a little girl. "My mummy's at work."

"So's mine."

Marty looked at Harry. He said, "They'd better come with us. My dad'll help them."

He said loudly, "My dad's vicar of St Margaret's. The church on the far side of the town square. Do you know it? If your mum's not at home follow us!"

"I don't know my way home," sniffled a small boy.

"That's OK. You come too. My dad will phone all your mums. Right. This way!" And he and Marty pushed through the kids and headed for Main Street.

The ground was still trembling.

"It's worse than the other night," said Harry.

Main Street was packed. People shouted. Women cried. A chimney pot rattled down a roof, causing the crowd to surge like water splashed by a stone.

"We'll never get through!" shouted Marty above the noise.

"We'll go this way!" Harry pointed to a gateway in an old brick wall on the same side of the street as Monk's Close; the children went through the gateway. They walked past the Almonry where waitresses had hurried outside into the garden.

"We can go out the other gate," shouted Harry, "into the cathedral grounds then past the cathedral and across the square. Everything's really shaking! Don't cry, you kids. We'll find your mums and dads! It's getting noisy! Yahoo!" he shouted merrily, and some little faces tried to smile. "Come on! Keep up! You'll need to carry that one," he told Marty, and Marty scooped up a tiny boy and he clung to her neck, his eyes wide with fear.

"This way." Harry led them through the gate to the cathedral grounds and past the bench where Marty had run away from Miss Hope. "Here's the cathedral! Keep looking up," he said to Marty.

"Falling pinnacles," she answered.

"If I say RUN!" yelled Harry, "you kids run. You understand?" He kept glancing up.

"Yes," pittered back at him.

They hurried alongside the cathedral.

The noise had grown – like a deep note played on a gigantic church organ, thought

Harry. He remembered the stone of the cathedral trembling to the sound of the organ when he and Marty had been inside the wall.

The sound, he realized, was coming *from* the cathedral.

Dust made him blink. The kids were rubbing their eyes, and crying louder.

"Keep going, you nuisances!" shouted Harry cheerfully.

He glanced up. The dust was being shaken from the dizzy heights of the cathedral. He saw dust spurt suddenly, way up near the sky, and exactly above the children.

He yelled, "RUN!" and every child ran. They raced, screaming and weeping, as Harry kept yelling, "RUN! RUN! STOP!" They stopped, and they looked back because Harry was looking back. A man was falling down the cathedral wall.

He was made of stone.

A statue.

He struck the grass with his shoulder, and broke in two at the waist. Dust shook itself down after him.

The whole huge cliff of stone which was the cathedral, vibrated.

The air around the cathedral vibrated, so that the dust shivered as if held in a trembling breeze – only it wasn't a breeze. It was—

"It's the noise!" said Harry.

"Get moving!" gasped Marty, clutching the

132

tiny boy.

"It's the sound!" shouted Harry. "It's the cathedral!"

"What?"

"It's not an earthquake! It's the engines! Don't you see? The cathedral is their ship! The organ is the noise that gives it energy! They use noise like we use rocket fuel! That's why the grass was tucked under the cathedral wall! When they tested the engines on Saturday night, *the cathedral rose off the ground*!"

CHAPTER TWENTY-TWO

They fled, Harry, and Marty carrying the little boy, and the kids. They fled alongside the cathedral because they could not get into Main Street through Monks Close for people coming and going.

They ran to the square where more people stood gaping at the gigantic building.

The first person Harry saw was Midge.

Harry gasped, "This way you kids!" and some of the children stayed with him while others vanished into the crowd in panic.

Midge grabbed Harry and lifted him. He put him down. He said, "Hi, Marty," as if nothing much was happening. "I'll take him if you like." Midge took the tiny boy and patted him. "I can see Dad. And Mum. And Jennie's somewhere."

"I'm here," said Jennie, as she popped from behind Midge. "Some first day at school for me," she said, her face whiter than ever.

"Me too," said Marty. "More or less. What a noise! Harry thinks the cathedral's the giants' space ship."

Midge nodded as if he had already guessed that. It was obvious that the sound was coming from the cathedral.

People were holding their ears. The crowd moved back from the cathedral.

"The whole thing's shaking!" cried Midge and people backed away further.

Cries and weeping rose above the thrum of sound which poured from the cathedral.

They waited. Harry found himself crouching as if ready to run, and he looked around and he saw many people crouching, not knowing they were doing it, then...

"The door's opening!" gasped Marty, and the cries of the crowd faded, and out of the great door stepped the giants.

*　　*　　*　　*　　*

They stood, the giants, close to the door. More came out.

"Miss Hope," said Harry to himself. And it *was* Miss Hope. But a Miss Hope twice as tall as Midge.

"And Miss Jackdaw."

Dad's hand landed on Harry's shoulder. "There's your head teacher."

"And the two men from the bookshop," said Midge.

"And the toyshop man!" gasped Jennie.

"That's the woman who kept me from putting my hat on straight," cried Mum. "Aren't they big? Oh, I don't feel well! Why are they so big? Why are they that size?"

"Hang on, Mum," warned Midge. "Jen, are you all right? Miss Hope's raised her hand. She's going to say something. Listen! Quiet!" shouted Midge, and his voice fled across the crowd, silencing people who had dared to speak.

"You have found us out."

Miss Hope's voice sounded the same as in the classroom, thought Harry.

"Leave us alone!" shouted a man in the crowd.

"Some of you have seen us as we really are – as you all see us now..."

The man who had shouted was at the front of the crowd, close to one of the paths which cut through the grass of the square. He bent down.

"We knew it would happen one day..."

"He's got a brick!" gasped Harry.

The man threw the brick towards Miss Hope, but it landed short and rolled up to her feet.

Miss Hope looked at the brick, then shrugged at the other giants.

136

"He's got another brick!" said Harry. "He's pulling them out of the path!"

"We do not wish to leave..." Miss Hope gestured at the cathedral above her, "...but we know what you are like–"

"And we know what you're like!" yelled the man. "You're a monster! Take that!"

He threw the second brick.

"Leave her alone!" screamed Harry.

The brick hit the cathedral wall, but the sound of it striking was lost in the great deep voice of the ancient stones.

"We came here," cried Miss Hope, "a thousand years ago!"

"Go home!"

Another brick flew.

"We do not wish to go home."

"Go home!" rose from the crowd.

"No!" screamed Harry. "Don't go!"

Miss Hope turned. She looked straight at Harry.

"Don't go!" he shouted. Dad's hand tightened on his shoulder.

"We do not wish to go!" Miss Hope's voice rose so that the crowd quietened.

Even at a distance, Harry could tell that Miss Hope was weeping. All the giants were sad.

"We do not wish to go home," said Miss Hope again, "for the same reason that you would not wish to go home if you had gone to

a distant shore and settled. You would not go
– and leave your children…?"

Miss Hope was asking a question.

She waited. Was she expecting an answer?

"I see that you do not understand." She
raised her hand helplessly.

"We do not wish to leave *our* children. Our
generations of children who live only seventy
or so years on this planet, like other human
beings. Don't you see?" Miss Hope raised
both hands, so that she was pleading, and tears
fell from her eyes. "All you mothers and
fathers. All you grandmothers and grand-
fathers. All of you, for a thousand years back,
you are our children!"

Then she stared straight at Harry.

He stepped forward.

Miss Hope touched one hand to her lips and
waved.

Harry waved back.

Then Miss Hope turned away.

A brick struck her leg. The other giants
caught her and hurried her through the great
door of the cathedral.

"No!" cried Harry. "Leave them alone!" he
screamed. He tried to run to the cathedral, but
Dad's hand held him, and Midge held him.

The voice of the cathedral deepened. Dust
piled down.

The ground shook so fiercely that Harry
staggered.

People ran, screaming.

"Come on!" gasped Dad. "You kids run!" He grabbed Mum's arm.

They ran.

They fled across the square after the crowd, the tiny boy sobbing in Midge's arms. The children who had followed Harry ran away with the crowd.

As they reached the cannon the note from the cathedral changed, and they hesitated.

They held their ears.

"Get behind the cannon!" shouted Dad. He pushed Mum down, the cannon between her and the cathedral.

"Hang on, you two!" yelled Midge, and Harry and Marty clung to the cannon's wheels, their arms through the spokes.

The massive tower of the cathedral vibrated so that it became blurred.

The great walls blurred.

Harry saw a black line, which was a shadow, appear under the bottom edge of the walls.

"It's rising!" he shrieked. "It's taking off!"

The air shook around the vast building, and the black line grew wider as the cathedral rose.

Midge seemed to guess what was about to happen, because when Harry let go of the cannon and stood up, Midge caught him and dragged him into his arms so that the tiny boy's cries filled his ears; but he stared round at the cathedral as the huge mass rose until daylight was underneath it.

"Hang on tight!" howled Midge. "She's going!"

And the cathedral went.

It vanished upwards so swiftly that by the time Harry blinked, it had gone. Then he found out why Midge had told them to hang on.

A wind screamed and struck the backs of their heads. Marty's mouth opened, and Harry knew she was shrieking in terror, but her voice was lost in the tremendous noise of the wind which rushed towards where the cathedral had stood. And things flew in the wind: a whole storm of leaves and, amid the leaves, clothing, and bicycles and flying bodies, and scraps of plastic and paper...

Harry thought that perhaps a bang big enough to fill the world deafened him for half a minute, but he was so dazed that he couldn't be certain.

Then silence smothered the town.

Silence lay on top of the town as heavily as a blanket.

Harry rolled free of Midget's grasp.

His mum and dad were blinking and touching each other's faces.

Marty still clung, as if frozen, to the wheel of the cannon.

The tiny boy was staring with enormous eyes at the wreckage strewn across the square, and at the gigantic dark shape on the earth which was the exact shape of the cathedral – the shape that had landed a thousand years before, and now had gone because the people who had built that shape – the giants – had run away to the stars, because – oh, because, thought Harry – because they were afraid of their children.

CHAPTER TWENTY-THREE

A year passed.

The shape of the cathedral remained sharp and clear, for it was being turned into a garden by the people of the town.

Dad had said that they should be ashamed of their fear and violence.

And some were ashamed enough to work on the garden; and others worked in memory of the giants who had been their friends and teachers. Though many still talked of monsters and what a lucky escape for humanity when the monsters left.

"There's no arguing with some people," Midge had said.

Midge had spent hours on the roof of the Almonry, replacing tiles and chimneys dragged off by the wind which had rushed in to fill the space with such a BANG! seconds after the cathedral had vanished.

"Oh, well, you know, the Almonry was probably built by the giants. It's reckoned to be a thousand years old. Though – come to think of it – half the town was probably built by them, because they were always here, helping us."

And he had nodded at Jennie who was mixing cement, and he grinned down at Marty and Harry who were passing up tiles.

He said, "Watch out for falling moss, you nuisances. And let's have those tiles, quick as you like! The sooner this old Almonry opens again, the sooner we can all sit down in peace, and scoff our coffee and cream doughnuts!"

He grinned at Jennie, who blushed.

Marty blew a kiss to Harry who also blushed, and he was so embarrassed that he didn't know what to do with the tile in his hand. So he dropped the tile, and walked away a little bit.

Then Marty's feet ran after him. Her lips landed, soft and warm on his cheek, startling a yell out of him.

Midge and Jennie laughed.

And Marty laughed.

Harry grinned through his blushes.

Really! Giants were one thing.

But girls—!

THE GHOSTS OF RAVENS CRAG
by Hugh Scott

It begins on the motorway. The Smiths –
Mum and Dad, Sammy, Miff (the narrator)
and baby Bertie – are on their way to the
Lake District, when they pass an old man
in a brown suit, standing on the verge,
smiling...
Then, on the slip road, they pass him again
... and again... On arrival at their holiday
destination, *The Ravens Crag Hotel*, the
Smiths soon find themselves drawn in to a
dark supernatural mystery, involving a
boxed-in pew at the local church, a Devil-
worshipping child-murderer and the ghosts
of dead children. And to be drawn in is to
be in danger. Deadly danger...

"Horror and good writing don't often go
hand in hand – Scott is a master of the
genre." *The Sunday Telegraph*

THE HAUNTED SAND
by Hugh Scott

"Murder, Frisby! Murder on the beach!"

There's something creepy in the church-yard. There's something deathly down on the sand. Darren feels it, Frisby hears it, George thinks it's a bit of a laugh. But there's nothing funny about murder...

"Intriguing ingredients abound: a haunted church; fearful chases; ghostly weeping; skulls; bronze helmets; gems and the Black Death... Rendellesque subtleties of story-line build to an unforeseen climax." *The Times Educational Supplement*

"An unmissable book." *Books for Keeps*

MISTER SPACEMAN
by Lesley Howarth

Thomas Moon is a space freak. His room's done up like the MIR Space Station. He hunts the web-sites daily for space news and stories. He wants to be an astronaut. And according to the mysterious email he's just received, addressed to Mister Spaceman, his dreams are about to come true.

"Each of her books is an invigorating display of verbal fireworks, and a fresh foray into the imagination." *Gillian Cross, TES*

MAPHEAD
by Lesley Howarth

Greetings from the Subtle World –

Twelve-year-old MapHead is a visitor from the Subtle World that exists side by side with our own. Basing himself in a tomato house, the young traveller has come to meet his mortal mother for the first time. But, for all his dazzling alien powers, can MapHead master the language of the human heart?

"Weird, moving and funny by turns... Lesley Howarth has a touch of genius."
Chris Powling, Books for Keeps

"Offbeat and original... Strongly recommended to all who enjoy a good story."
Books For Your Children

JET SMOKE AND DRAGON FIRE
by Charles Ashton

"The dragon roared, and roared again; and mingling with the smoke left by the aeroplane, the dragon's flame went spinning and coiling."

The odd thing about Sparrow's village is that although it has all the gadgets of the modern world – telephones, televisions, calculators – no one knows how they work. But this mystery is nothing to the extraordinary events that transform the lives of Sparrow and his friends after an encounter with the magical Puckel and, of course, with the dragon itself...

"A superb writer... Sensationally good."
The Sunday Telegraph

"A racy story full of fantastic adventures."
Junior Education

TO SUMMON A SPIRIT
by Enid Richemont

Jessica Jenkins feels strangely troubled.

Memories flit through her head like moths, but which of them are real? Sick with glandular fever, she remembers moving house, the arguments between Ma and Dad, the woods where she found refuge and the girl from the past who called her "a spirit". But did *the girl* summon Jess or did Jess summon *her*?

Sliding between the present day and Victorian times, Jess finds a new friend but also makes some shocking discoveries in this intriguing time-slip story.

THEY MELTED HIS BRAIN!
by Simon Cheshire

Schoolboy film-director Matthew Bland makes sensational movies.

With titles such as *Head Transplant*, they all star his friends Lloyd and Julie… and they're all rubbish. But one morning, at a quarter past three, Matthew's video records a sinister, brain-washing TV transmission that's beyond even *his* wildest imaginings! Can Matthew Bland, investigative film-maker, expose the evil doers before the final credits roll?

Fab, funny, fast and furious – these are just a few words that begin with the letter F. Do they describe this book? You'll have to read it and make up your own mind!

WHATEVER HAPPENED TO KATY-JANE?
by Jean Ure

"That's not me! That's not me!" She hurled the book across the floor. "It's not me!"

Waking in hospital after a road accident, Katy-Jane quickly realizes that something is not right; in fact, many things are wrong. The strange mousy woman by her bedside claims to be her mum; but her mum died over a year ago. She has different friends too, and different likes and interests – she even looks different. And yet she feels the same. How can she be Katy-Jane and not Katy-Jane? Whatever can have happened to her? And, most important of all, will she ever again be the person she once was? Jean Ure's gripping story is full of mystery and suspense.

MORE WALKER PAPERBACKS

For You to Enjoy